Lady Violet Greville

Keith's Wife

Vol. II

Lady Violet Greville

Keith's Wife
Vol. II

ISBN/EAN: 9783337065379

Printed in Europe, USA, Canada, Australia, Japan

Cover: Foto ©Andreas Hilbeck / pixelio.de

More available books at **www.hansebooks.com**

KEITH'S WIFE.

A Novel.

BY

LADY VIOLET GREVILLE,

AUTHOR OF

"ZOE," "FAITHS AND FASHIONS," ETC.

IN THREE VOLUMES.
VOL. II.

LONDON:
RICHARD BENTLEY AND SON,
Publishers in Ordinary to Her Majesty the Queen.
1883.
[All Rights Reserved.]

CONTENTS OF VOL. II.

KEITH'S WIFE.

CHAPTER I.

LOVING.

T was morning—the morning of the twenty-ninth of May; a morning as bright and clear as the tender rose of Dorothy's cheek or the smile that haunted the corner of her curving lips. She sat silently beside her husband while the carriage rolled towards the station, her hand clasped in his, and the strange sense of possession, which seems a woman's first impression of marriage, pervading her entirely. It was as if she had passed from her own existence into that of another—some new, vaguely delightful existence, joyous, and full of eager hope.

As they passed down the drive, where the
dew still lay heavy on the fresh young grass,
and the browsing deer lifted their slim heads
to stare, and then, with a pretence of fear, suddenly bounded away ; as they passed through
the lodge by the courtesying woman, and along
the lanes redolent of new-mown hay and haw-
thorn blossoms ; as they turned their backs on
the familiar village and the Angel House,
surrounded by its many-coloured lichen-
clothed wall, and on all the sights and sounds
of her childhood, finally reaching the tiny
deserted station, where a few countrywomen
waited with baskets on their arms for the
coming of the train—Dorothy realized, to her
surprise, that she felt no pang of regret, no
tremor of doubt, such as had assailed her on
her wedding eve.

Safe in her husband's arms, his caresses had
transported her into another region ; like the
kiss wakening the princess in the fairy-tale,
Keith's love had made all her previous experiences wax faint and far away, leaving only
the promise of a more intensely vivid existence in the future. The numerous pin-pricks
that had given her such acute pain—Mrs.
Maynard's insinuations, Margaret's half-en-
vious sneers, Mrs. Strait's cruel indifference—

all evaporated, sinking into welcome in-significance in her mind. Keith loved her; Keith was hers.

She looked with a tender wonder at all the paraphernalia of a fashionable young man's requirements—at the mountain of rugs and coats, at the large dressing-bag set full of silver-topped bottles and ivory brushes, the cigarette-cases of various hues and shapes, the railway lamp and key, the luncheon-basket, and the variety of articles which her little head had never before troubled itself to imagine.

Keith, after asking permission, lighted a cigar (Dorothy wondered that she had never before noticed how peculiarly pleasant and aromatic was the smell of tobacco smoke), and now sat still in his corner of the railway carriage, in an evident condition of quiescent well-being. Dorothy, close beside him, feasted her eyes on his appearance. In the days of her courtship she had scarcely dared to lift her eyes and study his features deliberately; but now, now that he was her very own, her treasure and her care, she noted every curve and line, and trick of speech or manner.

How his mind showed itself, even in his clothes, she thought, which were so neat, so well-chosen, so simple; how easily the grey

shooting-suit fell about his well-shaped limbs;
with what careless grace he held his cigar,
when turning suddenly and catching her
wistful eyes fixed upon him, he smiled lovingly
back at her.

'Have we everything, dear?' he said
kindly. 'I hope le Goui put in all your
things; you see, I scarcely know them by
sight yet.'

'Le Goui has forgotten nothing, I think.
What a capital servant he is; has he been
long with you, Keith?'

'Years!' said Keith lazily, stretching out
his fingers in search of Dorothy's hand, which
had slidden under her cloak. 'He always
treats me like a child that knows nothing,
and is quite furious if I dare to insinuate that
he may have made a mistake. He will adopt
you as another child now, I suppose, so you
really need not disturb yourself about anything.'

'I have only the travelling-bag you gave
me and my rug and ulster,' said Dorothy,
thinking how delightful it was to owe everything to the handsome man beside her, and to
feel like a beggar-maid lifted into the light of
a new King Cophetua's generosity.

Keith's gifts had not been many hitherto,

but though few in number they were well-chosen and costly: the dressing-case and sundry family diamonds and necessary jewels he intended to purchase and have reset on their arrival in London.

'Are you sure the maid will meet you at the hotel to-night?' Keith demanded, with solicitude. 'I cannot have *my wife* without a maid, compelled to go down on her knees to pack boxes, and to ask the chambermaid for charily rendered services.'

'It is all right, I believe. I am sure Trimmer—that is her name—understood perfectly; but you know, Keith, I am accustomed to do everything for myself. I have never had a maid.'

'We have changed all that, however, now, dear; my darling is never to fatigue herself or be worried again.'

'How good you are to me, Keith!' Dorothy laid her head on his shoulder, pressing closer to him, with the endearing action of a child. 'How am I ever to repay you for all you have done?'

'By being my own dear lovely wife. Dorothy, do you know I think you are the most beautiful woman I ever saw in my life; you will make a sensation at Venice.'

'But, Keith'—Dorothy spoke very low, and stroked his hand gently as she spoke— 'you don't care about my making a sensation; you don't value me only for my beauty, do you? You love me just because I am myself, your faithful, worshipping, devoted little love. Say yes, dear.'

Keith laughed.

'How sentimental women are, to be sure! I never credited you with half the amount of airy fancies you possess. I thought you were a little cold at first—a trifle of a *bas-bleu.* I am glad you are not; women of flesh and blood and ordinary feelings are far pleasanter to associate with.'

'I don't know if my feelings are ordinary; I only know that I never seem to have lived till I met you, and that you are all the world to me. I can conceive nothing beyond or above you; you bound my very horizon, Keith—my thoughts, my time, my life are yours.'

'Sweetly spoken, little one,' and he kissed her on the upturned lips; 'but you must keep those kind of speeches for me, remember. Don't talk like that before the world; people might laugh; sentiment is always sneered at in society. *I* like it, you understand, immensely; the very simplicity of it makes its especial charm—but keep your love hidden.'

'People would laugh at a wife's love for her husband! Oh, Keith, what can the world of fashion be, then?'

He smiled at the scared look in her expressive eyes.

'Don't be afraid, dear; they will not laugh at you, I promise you, for I shall be there.'

'Keith, do you love me—really and truly, I mean, with all your heart and soul, as I do?'

'Certainly. Have I not proved it?'

'By marrying me? I suppose so; but yet it seems to me as if some natures absorbed all the passion of others to feed their own life, and yet could not respond in kind. Of course they are wonderfully exceptional natures. You are all that, Keith, and thus I feel as if you never *could* love me as I love you, and then I begin to doubt; I am so very unworthy.'

'Don't doubt.' He pinched her cheek kindly.

'You have had everything; you must have loved and been loved. I cannot even hope to be your first love; it is so hard that a woman *never* can come first.'

'I never loved anyone as I do you,' he responded, a little hoarsely.

'I know. I am—I try to be satisfied, dear, and yet it seems to me as if I never *could* be satisfied. I thirst for all you can give me.'

'I have given you riches; to be rich is the best of all things—don't you think so?'

'It is very nice to be rich, of course—delightful,' and Dorothy looked again at the magnificent fur rug, and the dressing-bag with its massive fittings, and at the rings on her finger, and remembered her new maid and le Goui, and chid herself sharply for being ungrateful; then, with a swing of true sentiment, breaking in on the artificial appraisement of novelty and ease, 'But for all that, Keith, it is better to be loved; I would rather have that than all.' And down went her little fair, trim head (from which she had removed the velvet hat in order to be more at ease) upon his arm, while she burrowed her face in the woolly material of his sleeve. Keith thought it all very nice, very new and very innocent. Dorothy's loving speeches had a flavour of Arcadian simplicity; they reminded him of boyish feelings, of curds and cream, and snowy lambs with their necks tied up in blue ribbons. He had no objection to being adored, for the serene devotion that shone in his wife's gentle eyes proved a piquant con-

trast to the hackneyed allurements of more
skilled and worldly women. There is, of
course, the ripe charm of experience, throwing
a borrowed glamour over the most ordinary
emotions, and carefully heightening the dull
and irresponsive faculties; but to a man of the
world there is even a greater charm in the
awkwardness of first love, as it stumbles into
expression and ignorantly shows its hand,
keeping no artifices in reserve, but the constant surprises afforded by the outpourings of
a rich and lavish nature seeking to spend
itself in love, and humbly waiting to be
taught the unfamiliar lesson.

' Keith, if we continue to love one another
like this, it seems to me that our affection will
grow and grow, and permeate our life until
earth will be turned into heaven. Is joy as
exhausting as sorrow ?'

' No, darling, joy is never exhausting; it is
like the silver sparkles of a fountain springing
up perpetually and never drooping or ceasing
so long as the water, the feeder of its life,
remains. Joy is a tonic. And you, my
Dorothy, are going to have an immense
quantity of joy. Have you ever thought of
your first impressions of Italy—of what you
will feel there ?'

'I have sometimes tried to picture to myself the scenes of which I have read—the vines, the cream-coloured oxen ploughing, the peasants, the blue sky which seems deeper and clearer the more you look into it, and what a writer has called the " caressing Italian sunshine;" but it is only a dream, imagination surely never can come up to reality.'

'Ah, well, you shall see it all, Dorothy; and I will teach you which are the things most worthy of admiration, and show you the best pictures and greatest works of art. I am a connoisseur in bric-à-brac, and I know every shop in Venice.'

'How delightful! One should always travel, I think, with a person who has lived in the country, and is versed in the ways of the people and understands their spirit. Ordinary travellers, who only put up at inns and talk to their couriers, must miss the whole gist and sense of travelling.'

'Quite true. I am sure we shall travel profitably ; it will be an unconventional *voyage de noce*, let us hope. Meanwhile, here we are. Put on your hat, dear, quickly; and let us try not to look like a honeymoon couple, or we shall attract much unnecessary attention.'

Notwithstanding Keith's precautions, the pair created considerable interest wherever they appeared. The handsome, intellectual-looking man, and the lovely girl leaning on his arm, were not ordinary travellers; and in the waiting-rooms, in the passages of hotels, on board the steamers, and in all the crowded haunts which the exigencies of travel necessitated their entering, they received a fair amount of stares and curious glances from the public. At last, after dazed impressions of smoky London; after hours of brisk and whirling movement, of a heaving, sullen, foamy sea, of bright and delectable Paris, with its hypocritical smiles and frivolous happiness, and the deep pathetic and turbulent misery hidden beneath; after flashes of minute French landscapes, with their long poplar-bordered roads, and their tiny villages crowned by the eternal steeple, and the blue-bloused peasants driving cattle to market; after visions of muddy, rushing rivers, and mountains, and flower-covered banks—Dorothy caught her first glimpse of Italy—her first sight of the wonderful tints of green, painted as with a magic pencil, and the lavish loving luxuriance of twining vine and acacia, bending willow and waving grass, and the fields

of roses. Her eyes travelled from this restful
chromatic scale of emerald to the sapphire of
Italian Alps, to the rosy snow-peaks and the
delicate azure sky, and suddenly the thought
came to her that hitherto the charm of
colour had been hidden from her knowledge.
They stayed a few days in the quaint old-
world cities of Northern Italy, with their high
narrow houses and overhanging ironwork,
their grass-grown streets brightened unexpectedly by little bits of brilliant drapery
hanging out of the windows, or by pots of
crimson carnations, with heavy drooping heads,
set on subtly-carved balconies; Dorothy thinking of Romeo and Juliet, and of the sweet old
passionate love-story—thinking that she too,
like the Veronese maiden, had felt the swift
lightning-touch of first love, had said from
her full heart:

> ' My bounty is as boundless as the sea,
> My love as deep ; the more I give to thee,
> The more I have, for both are infinite.'

Thrice happier and more fortunate she,
who, unlike Juliet, possessed her own true
love for ever. But over such scenes and
memories, with which her schoolgirl mind
was charged, Keith would not let her linger ;
he thirsted for the day and hour when he

could install his bride in his palace at Venice. He forgot, however, that the first impression created by the Queen of the Adriatic is scarcely the happiest. Like the most refined kind of beauty, which leaves the careless beholder at first sight unmoved, and requires familiarity for its perfect appreciation, so Venice, after a moment of comparative disappointment, gradually tightens its hold on the imagination and the affections, until residence in the fairy city becomes a passion. The gondolas looked black and gloomy to Dorothy; the waters of the canal dull and sluggish; the palaces dark and frowning; and even a damp drizzle was falling when they arrived, as if to remind them of England.

Keith cared nothing for this. He beamed with delight as he handed her out of his own private gondola. He led her across the threshold of a handsome building, over the door of which hung a massive gilt lantern, and said, staying his steps in the large painted vestibule: 'Welcome home, Dorothy.'

Notwithstanding his kind words, a shiver ran through her; it was as though some heavy cloud of darkness—some chill omen of unhappiness—had descended upon her. Keith noticed her shiver.

' Are you cold—perhaps the hall is chilly ?
Come up to your own room ; I ordered a
fire there, in case you might like it.'

They mounted the vast marble stairs, and
passed through a heavily gilded door, on each
side of which stood two black and gold statues
of negro boys bearing lamps, into a long
gallery hung with mirrors and large oil-
pictures. Their footsteps echoed sadly down
the parquet flooring ; and their two dusty
figures were reflected in a million fantastic
shapes and sizes in the numerous looking-
glasses.

' At night,' thought Dorothy, ' I should be
afraid here ;' and she clung more tightly to
her husband's arm.

At the end of the long gallery there was
a large drawing-room, also richly decorated
with paintings, gildings, and mirrors, and
furnished with stiffly arranged satin-covered
chairs and sofas. They passed again through
another and smaller apartment, into a room
fitted up in somewhat more modern fashion,
and evidently intended for intimate use. A
fire of wood-logs burnt on the low hearth, a
couple of easy-chairs stood near, and the
tables were heaped with a profusion of bowls
and vases of flowers—chiefly roses.

'This is your own room,' Keith said, walking to the window, and pushing aside the heavy brocade curtains to admit the distant view of the broadening waters of the Gran Canale, and the setting sun gilding the dome of St. Maria della Salute; 'and next here is your bedroom, and beyond it my rooms, which lead on to the grand staircase from the opposite direction. You perceive the palace forms a complete square. Shall you be at home here? Do you think you shall like it, dear? I hope so.'

'It is very magnificent,' Dorothy said with a sigh, sitting down on one of the brocaded sofas. 'I never saw so many beautiful objects together before in my life.'

A proud smile passed over Keith's handsome features.

'No; I flatter myself I have some fine things. See, here is a silver casket, worked by Cellini; here an old dagger, which may have belonged to one of the Doges; that picture is a Titian; this is a marvellously beautiful specimen of a Florentine table; and that ivory and ebony cabinet is in the best possible taste. I have put all the gems of my collection here for you, Dorothy.'

She murmured her thanks, but the grandeur

and the silence of the large empty spaces oppressed her. Hitherto, not even a servant had approached. True, she saw two men in black livery silently bowing in the vestibule when they arrived, but they had not reappeared; and le Goui and Trimmer were still engaged in looking after the luggage. There was a feeling of unreality about everything; she seemed to herself like one of the princesses in Hans Andersen's fairy-tales.

Keith now left her, saying he must speak to le Goui; and she determined to penetrate into her bedchamber, thinking to find there at least some trace of familiar home-comfort. She lifted the curtain; between each room there hung some heavy draperies, which, drowning all the usual sounds of domestic life, produced a deeper sense of solitude.

The room was panelled with tapestry, beautiful and rare even to her unaccustomed eyes; and the bed was a marvel of gigantic size and skilled carving. The hangings were of rich crimson and gold brocade; the quilt of yellow satin sewn with lilies, and bordered with deep lace of an old ecclesiastical design. The carved and gilt dressing-table supported a set of old silver caskets and bottles of quaint and curious shapes. On one side of the room, a large carved mirror reached to the floor; and, opposite it, a smaller mirror, framed in silver, and divided into panels, was suspended over the mantelshelf.

As Dorothy stood motionless with clasped hands in the middle of the room, her little grey figure (she was dressed in her favourite grey, the colour having seemed most appropriate even for a bride's travelling costume) glassed like some faint-hued water-colour, each line correctly rendered in the tall mirrors, she seemed an image of asceticism amidst the gorgeous splendour of her surroundings. Meanwhile, her thoughts swung idly to and fro — mentally comparing her past and present.

The Angel House with its fittings was faded, antiquated, and mellowed by time; the Queen Anne carvings and the panelled walls, the washed-out chintzes and the spindly-legged tables, the bits of old Chinese porcelain, collected when Chinese crockery was a fashion, were certainly relics of a by-gone age, but held no sad memories; they were relics of men and women who had lived and suffered, and spent their whole time in quiet domestic happiness. A homeliness and simplicity seemed to speak from their lips, which was lacking in the cold stateliness of the beautiful objects around her.

Men and women must have lived in the Venetian palace too ; yet she could only realize them as ghosts—as wall-pictures, or figments of her fancy. Her own little bedroom at the Angel House, with the rose-patterned dimity hangings, and the roses themselves nodding in on a summer's morning, and giving her a fragrant welcome ; the worn old armchair, covered with chintz, in which she had sat reading or thinking so many, many a time ; the little bookshelf of common deal, painted by her own hands, and filled with her favourite authors—her Keats, her Shakespeare, her Goldsmith, her Dickens, and, most prized of all, her little well-thumbed, red-leather 'Imitation.' How dear the memory of those common articles seemed to her as, clinging like a weary mariner in the ocean of empty splendour around her to the one little touch of home and childhood, she remembered all these things.

Glancing round in search of some familiar object, she noticed a large silver-clasped and bound prayer-book on the centre table, covered by an old silk cloth edged with faded gold braid, and adorned by four tarnished gold tassels. She seized the book eagerly. Here, at last, was something homelike—the words of prayer could never be strange, under whatever clime, and must prove a link to bind the exile to her country. She quickly unloosed the heavy clasps. The book was empty! It was only a curious old missal-case. She dashed it angrily on the table, and walked to the window. Empty!—like everything else around her— only sham magnificence, with no heart in it. At that instant, there came a sound of footsteps, and the servants appeared with the luggage : le Goui, smiling and oily as usual; Trimmer, fatigued and somewhat cross, permitting herself to be ordered hither and thither in a fashion no English maid who respected herself would for an instant have submitted to in her own country, or had she been less dazed and tired.

Keith came in their rear.

' Don't stay here, dear,' he said, with anxious solicitude ; ' you might catch cold—see, the window is open. Close it at once, le Goui, Madame may feel cold; and have the fire lighted.'

' I am not cold,' Dorothy said ; but her pale face and pinched look belied her.

Keith drew her away into her sitting-room, closed the door, settled her comfortably in an armchair, and took his place on a stool at her feet, pressing her two little icy hands in his.

'My little northern flower feels the cold more than I should have expected,' he said. 'See, I have not forgotten your predilections—the fire is bright enough, and the room is full of flowers. I remembered how sweet the Angel House always smelt of lilies.'

'You sent us those—they were *your* lilies—all I have is yours, Keith. Oh! shall I ever make you happy?—say!'

CHAPTER II.

VENICE.

DOROTHY awoke late on the morrow, wondering where she was; and glancing first with astonishment at the high bed and canopy of brocade which arched her head, seeming to reach almost to the ceiling, presently leant back with a feeling of delicious repose on the large downy pillows adorned with a large embroidered cypher in the corner and a frilling of deep lace.

The rest seemed delightful to her, after travelling for many days; and the knowledge that no further effort to dress hastily and catch a train was required of her was certainly extremely pleasant; but she missed Keith. Where had he gone, she wondered uncomfortably; the thought of his disappearance immediately gave her

a sensation of fear. She pulled the bell-rope
violently. Trimmer appeared in answer—as
English a figure as possible—with plain braided
white apron and neatly fitting gown. She
also had rested, and had had time to 'un-
pack some of her things, which was a blessing,'
she announced with a sniff to le Goui, the only
servant with whom, much to her chagrin, she
could converse—the others being Italians who
had never left their own country ; and 'thank
goodness I am not like any of those foreigners,
who never wash, and dine off messes,' she
added vindictively.

'Where is Mr. Chester ?' asked Dorothy,
from her bed.

'Gone out, madame ; and please, he said
you was to have chocolate as soon as you rang,
and breakfast at twelve.'

'At twelve! It must be very late—what
o'clock is it, then?'

'Only just ten o'clock, madame ; a decent
English breakfast-hour. I'll tell the housemaid
—Lauretta they call her—to bring your chocolate ; which, it seems, is all folks have for
breakfast here.'

Keith had gone out. Dorothy lay still and
thought : she did not feel hungry (though
when the dainty chocolate, on its silver tray,

was brought to her, the aromatic fumes soon gave her a desire to sip it), and needless to say, she thought of Keith. He was the great centre sun round which now all her ideas, like minor luminaries, revolved. How she could best please him, what, for the future, were to be her duties, her occupations, her privileges?—such were the problems that teazed her. It was evidently all so different from England. The very hours, the food, the lazy luxurious fashion of breakfasting in bed, spoke of a life of self-indulgence and ease. Where in *this* life was the space for duties ? In what way could she deny herself for him ? It seemed to her as if pleasure must be the be-all and end-all of this enchanted and wonderful existence.

What had become now of the stern views of duty and work—the earnest striving after knowledge and acquirement which had lashed her into energetic effort previous to her marriage ?

Keith invariably checked any tendency to ambition and study on her part ; he said women needed only to be charming and pretty, and sweet-tempered. Indeed, she could scarcely imagine the possibility of any outlet for her talents or her ambition in this splendid lotus-eating aspect of life.

Dorothy sighed, pushed her chocolate on

one side, and prepared to rise. Presently Keith knocked at her door. His bright, decided voice roused her from her dreams— seeming to infuse an element of manly life into the faded tapestry and heavy brocade hangings which still unwarrantably continued to oppress her.

'I am coming in a minute, Keith,' she said; at which she quickly motioned to Trimmer to fasten her gown.

That Keith should wait for her, that she should be inexcusably late, perhaps delay the luncheon, was certainly not the way to begin married life. Lady Darlington, she remembered, had particularly cautioned her against ordering bad dinners, or keeping men waiting for their food. Keith, however, was quietly seated in a large arm-chair reading the papers when she entered. He did not seem impatient or annoyed, but looked up amiably; she noticed this with a little quick tremor of happiness.

'Oh, Keith, I am so sorry to have kept you waiting.'

'It did not signify, dear. I only hope you had a good rest. Don't distress yourself about such a trifle; but, indeed, if you had really caused me inconvenience I should say the same. Mutual forbearance is absolutely necessary in

the married state. Why *should* you rise early
if you don't wish to? I can always breakfast
alone.'

'But Keith,' she said, looking shocked, 'I
would not let you breakfast alone for worlds;
why, I *like* to be with you—it is my duty and
my pleasure.'

'It is a pleasure to look at you in the early
morning, Dorothy; that pale blue stuff—what
do you call it?—is charming.'

'I am glad you like it.'

Dorothy had found it difficult to divest herself in a moment of her long established habits
of simplicity and thrift; almost all the dresses
of her trousseau were plain and of woollen
materials, much to the chagrin of little Miss
Clack, the dressmaker, who asserted that it
was 'all very well not to spoil the modesty of
a girl's composition, but that married ladies
must, above all, be elegant.' It was with
quite a little show of anger that the worthy
woman had noticed Dorothy set aside all the
richer and more costly silks and satins proffered
her, and choose neat and inexpensive materials.
Dorothy had felt the force of Miss Clack's
remarks since she had come into the grand
old Venetian palace; her willowy figure seemed
to her to shrink to such small and poor

dimensions; consequently her husband's commendation of the blue merino, which was her favourite gown, caused her unmitigated and welcome satisfaction.

'See what I bought for you in my morning walk,' Keith said, tossing a little box into her lap. 'I have not been idle, though you were such a sleepy little puss.'

Dorothy took from the box a ring of antique shape.

'What a beautiful stone; it shines like a star, and seems to catch all the rays of light.'

'It is a star ruby; they are rather rare, and thought to be lucky.'

'They must be lucky, they seem to have a soul in them—to be more than a mere jewel.'

'I am glad you like it. The morning was so fine, I strolled out, meaning to settle our plans for the day, and in one of the little shops on the Rialto I saw this, and thought at once you would like it. Are you fond of jewels?'

'Not in themselves, but jewels like this ring'—here Dorothy slipped it over her finger and looked admiringly at it—'seem so full of meaning, they attract and fascinate me beyond measure; pearls, too, I like—they are the perfection of form and purity.'

'Pearls stand for tears. You shall not have any, Dorothy.'

'Oh, please, Keith; I am not afraid.'

'Then you shall have the most beautiful necklace I can get; a matchless row of pearls. But let us go to breakfast now; my walk has given me an appetite.'

The dining-room in nowise fell short of the splendour of the other apartments; it was hung with old stamped leather, and had a ruddy sheen of gold about it. Jets of gold candelabra jutted out from the walls, and overhead hung one of those fairy crystal chandeliers, the delicate intricacy of which is such that it seems almost incredible as the work of ordinary human fingers.

The meal concluded, while they sat drinking the sweet Italian wine and nibbling at luscious figs and strawberries, Dorothy could distinguish the tideless lap of the waves against the stone bastions of the palace, and the distant monotonous cry of the gondoliers. Every instant she expected to hear a brisk clap of the hands, to see the scene, like one of the visions in the 'Arabian Nights,' disappear into blank space, and to find herself perhaps alone in her room at the Angel House, having discovered that Keith's presence, his love and

her marriage, were only evanescent dreams.
No such imaginative fancies tormented Mr.
Chester. For some years now he had been
accustomed to luxury, and, indeed, previously he had indulged, even on a small
income, in all the aids to a *dolce far niente* life
which the cheap and poetical surroundings of
a southern residence render possible, insomuch that though he accepted riches as a
matter of course, yet poverty or even middle-
class humdrumness would have appeared in-
tolerable to him. Discomfort being essentially
a question of habit, sybaritic indulgence had
become with Keith second nature. He liked
his palace, his treasures, and his bric-à-brac,
not because of their intrinsic value, but
because they ministered to his acquired and
imperative tastes. He appreciated his wife
more keenly because she did him honour,
because she pleased his fastidious refinement,
and satisfied his sense of beauty; also, perhaps, because she spoke in a clear low tone,
neither mumbling nor bawling, and studied
earnestly to fall in with his slightest wishes.
He would never have lived a day with a ter-
magant or wilful woman; yet it may be
questioned whether the gentle yielding love
with which his wife wrapped him round, as

in an atmosphere of southern scented breezes,
was the surest and best way of clinching his
regard for her. A faint suspicion of contempt,
the contempt of a selfish man who cannot fathom
the strength of love yielding its own will for
love's sake, tinctured the real affection he
entertained for her. She was a new element
of pleasure in his life and he thought to con-
ciliate her, like a child, by presents of jewels
and bonbons, and beautiful surroundings. He
judged her by himself; *he* would not have been
happy in a garret, and he scorned the notion
that Dorothy could have endured any fate
that necessitated sacrifice. How little we
know of the heart even of those we love best !
Keith acted according to his lights; he thought
himself, and indeed he strove to behave like,
the most devoted husband.

The remainder of this their first day in
Venice was passed by Dorothy in a dream of
happiness. She was not sufficiently learned
in art to know the difference of a Giotto or a
Botticelli, to understand the technical marvels
of Tintoretto's colouring in the Doge's Palace, or
to read strange allegorical meanings in quaint
presentments of purgatory and hell; but she
could shudder at the majestic and vivid con-
ceptions of a last judgment, and she could feel

the intense beauty of the Madonna's countenance in the glorious 'Assumption,' that
haunted her like a vision of heaven. She
could perceive the delicate purity of tone and
grace of gesture in a group of Luca della
Robbia's cool and spiritual white bas-reliefs;
and, best of all, she could surrender herself to
the charm of the Venetian life and climate as
she floated, towards evening, in a noiseless
gondola, nestling in her husband's arms, and
while the frail bark swept like some dim image
of night out into the wide golden-coloured
quivering waters, and sky and sea met in one
ruddy streak, the liquid notes of song sprang
upward in that passionate cry of love :

'Oh, Venezia benedetta, non ti posso piu
lasciar!'

The days passed like magic in a rapture of
love; Dorothy wishing only that time might
pause, that the hours of each day might
lengthen indefinitely—days which were all
dazzling sunshine, restful shadow and lingering flower-scents ; nights of moonlit heavens,
pricked with twinkling stars, their silence
cheered by the dim echo of some distant
lover's serenade. No aftertime could be so
beautiful again—so rich in wonders, so prolific
in grand and glorious sights.

Keith noticed her intelligently admiring countenance and felt satisfied. He could never be dull in company with a woman so sensitive to all the influences of art and beauty. He had, however, less sympathy with her enthusiastic raptures about the historic past, when, shuddering, her hand locked in his, they stood on the Bridge of Sighs; or else, when in the quickly moving gondola they cleft the deep shadows, and skirted the dank and moss-grown walls of prisons and palaces, she struggled, with all her energy, mentally to reconstruct the past.

'History is not half so interesting as our own story,' he would say; 'lovers were always lovers, and Doges were but men after all, and Shakespeare, we know, had probably never even seen a Jew.'

'Yet I like to think it was all true: that once there lived a real Jessica, a real Desdemona. I like to people these deserted palaces with living, breathing, happy creatures like ourselves. I like to think of the grand sea-fights, of the pomp and pride of the pearl of the Adriatic, of the stir and life of commerce, of the treasures brought from the east and the west, and collected in this one spot.'

'Not, of course, of the poor prisoners pining in the dungeons ?'

'Yes, most of all of them; of their poor broken hearts and their lonely sighs.'

'If you had your way, Dorothy, you would waste all your time in feeling for other people who have lived and died long ago, so that you would never have a thought to spare for me !'

'Don't you feel these things, too ?' His imputation of her indifference fell unheeded, she knew so utterly the falsehood of it. 'Doesn't your heart burn within you at the injustice and cruelty of men towards each other ?'

'I deeply feel the fact of having been cheated out of my money, and persuaded to buy a copy instead of an original picture, or a tinkered up instead of a genuine bit of silver; but I am thankful to say, that owing to that sad experience which, I fear, can only be dearly gained, I am seldom taken in now.'

'I was not speaking of buying pictures, though, of course, to be cheated must be very annoying; but when you hear or read tales of suffering and misery, does it not seem to take away for a time all your own happiness ?'

'Certainly not. If it is a dreary book, such

as makes women cry, I toss it away and light a
cigar; if it is a true story, I try not to think of it.
There are plenty of people ready and willing
enough to concern themselves with melancholy
things—doctors, lawyers, sick-nurses, religious
people, whose business it is to cultivate the
loathsome; let them do it, and leave me in
peace.'

'But, Keith, you are a Liberal, you are a
landlord yourself; you must surely occasionally find it necessary to decide, to act, to take
the initiative on subjects that are not personal?'

'How easy it is, dear, to perceive that you
had once begun to study for a Cambridge
examination! I scarcely fancy these are the
topics most brides linger over and talk about.
If you must know, then, I let people have all
the liberty they like, as far as is compatible
with my own. Is it not true, our liberty of
which we boast, political or theological, very
frequently consists only in curtailing other
people's liberty ? But the fact of my giving
others free scope does not mean that I am
to spend my life in their service. That
theological notion of self-sacrifice I look upon
as repugnant to the dignity of human nature,
and utterly mischievous.'

'But is it not the teaching of our Lord?'

'Palestine is not England,' said Keith lightly; 'and teachings—after all not intended in a literal sense—which were good for the Jews of that time, would scarcely stand the test of modern civilization.'

'Do you really mean that our Lord's teaching is obsolete?'

'No, not precisely. I will tell you, my feeling is that it would be perfectly impossible to carry out the views of the Bible, and I consider, therefore, all religious discussions a decided mistake: nothing produces ill-feeling so quickly. I don't want to solve theological quibbles with my wife. Shall we go and have an ice at Florian's, eh? You look quite fagged out with the result of your keen spirit of sight-seeing and argument.'

Dorothy acquiesced, confessed she was a little tired, feeling, indeed, that fatigue was but a trifle compared with the smallest divergence between her own and her husband's opinions, which necessitated the silent avoiding of a topic. He, it was evident, shied away from all arguments on principle; she, on the contrary, would gladly have pushed them to their extremest limits, content, if she then deemed her reasoning incorrect, to acknowledge her error with a proud joyfulness.

CHAPTER III.

STILL UNDER THE SPELL.

T was about the end of June, when, returning one day from a curiosity hunt among the shops of the Rialto, Dorothy found a card lying on the large marble-topped table in the vestibule, which felt charmingly pleasant and cool after the exertion of a hot walk and the annoyance of bargaining with vendors in a confined and stifling space. She lingered a moment, enjoying the welcome freshness, and holding the visiting-card between her finger and thumb.

'What is that?' said Mr. Chester, noticing her delay.

'Some lady's visiting-card,' she said.

'So I perceive. Whose is it?' Standing behind her, he read the name over her shoulder: 'Marchesa Bellaggio.'

Hitherto Dorothy had received no visitors, and, whether from fear of intruding or from ignorance of her arrival, very few cards had been left upon her, Mr. Chester, indeed, seeming indifferent as to the fact of her returning visits. In any case, she would have pleaded the natural timidity of a bride at encountering perfect strangers ; but in addition, she dreaded ceremonious calls still more from the fact of her imperfect acquaintance with the Italian language.

'The Marchesa Bellaggio !' repeated Keith. 'It is very kind of her to have called so soon ; she is one of the greatest ladies here, and frequently at the Court.'

'Indeed,' responded Dorothy indifferently, tossing off her hat as she settled herself luxuriously on the sofa in her own cool room.

The green jalousies effectually shut out all glare, and produced a most agreeable half-light.

'You must return the Marchesa's visit,' said Keith.

'Some day—yes.' Shyness overcame Dorothy at the very thought.

'No, directly—to-morrow, I mean. It is always done here. You must not offend a great lady at the very outset. Remember I have been in diplomacy, and know the current value of civility.'

'You said nothing about quickly returning the other cards ; you have not forgotten, surely, that there are several there in that china bowl ?'

'My child, you must learn to understand the various shades of society. Those other people did not signify ; the Marchesa is different.'

'Oh dear ! I shall never understand the importance of these trifles,' said Dorothy, in a desponding tone, fanning herself with a newspaper. 'How fortunate for me that I have you always by my side. After all, it is perhaps nicer than if I were very wise, and never needed your help.'

Keith stopped in his restless pacing up and down to kiss her gently on the upturned brow.

'Of course I shall help you, dear ; but you must soon learn to be wise yourself. Our honeymoon is over, Dorothy ; it has lasted nearly a month. We have been very happy, have we not ? We have had our pleasure ; now we must taste of some of the business of life.'

Dorothy caught at Keith's hand, which hung down beside the sofa, and pressed it to her lips.

'Is it really over? I hate to think that anything so perfect can be over. I *am* sorry.'

'So am I sorry,' and Keith, looking at the pure, pale profile while she kept her head bent over his hand, thought she was certainly a sweet creature, and felt proud that she was his own.

But presently he became more practical. You see, he was a man of the world; he had never before lived for so long a time in solitude (even though the solitude had been enlivened by the presence and love of a beautiful woman), and he longed to return to the companionship of other men.

'Yes, we will go to-morrow, Dorothy; in the afternoon, at the hour the Marchesa drinks coffee. Put on your blue dress; you look best in that, and, naturally, I should wish you to make a good impression.'

'I don't care what manner of impression I make upon strangers,' said Dorothy impatiently. 'What are they to me?'

'You are too unworldly, my dear. It is no doubt a pretty and unusual trait in a woman, but it gives rise to disappointments; it is better to be practical, and have a little common-sense. The world is not perfect, you and I are not perfect; but we shall get on far better by making the most of our advantages, and not expecting too much from other people. Meanwhile, try and please the Marchesa.'

The mere fact of being commanded to make one's self agreeable usually does away with the possibility of the effort ; and when, on the morrow, they landed at the foot of the marble steps leading up to the Bellaggio Palace, Dorothy felt almost paralyzed with timidity. Keith observed the slight twitching of her sensitive mouth, which he knew denoted agitation, and whispered to her, with a kind, strong pressure of her hand, the words : ' Courage, dear ; don't be afraid.'

The Marchesa's palace was as large and as magnificent as their own (indeed, it seemed to Dorothy as if to be lodged poorly were the exception, rather than the rule, at Venice), and the servant led them through several antechambers and galleries before they finally reached the room—a moderate-sized octagon, hung with dark-red satin and garnished in each corner with tall looking-glasses set in white and gold frames, thus effectually dispensing with angles—where their hostess sat conversing with a friend.

The Marchesa was a remarkable-looking woman, of tall stature, with a head like a sphinx. She had chiselled features, her eyes were magnificent, full of coquettish languor; her mouth, though somewhat large, was expressive, and her complexion resembled clear ivory. She was dressed in a loose robe of tawny yellow, with some kind of wide soft sash carelessly knotted at the waist; and as she spoke she played with a large cream-coloured fan, on which were painted trailing roses, opening and shutting it regularly The little dark man to whom she was speaking had a very brown skin, and a face like a monkey. He used a great deal of animated gesticulations with his speech, bowed very low at the arrival of Mr. and Mrs. Chester, stared rather rudely at the latter, and then resumed his seat and endeavoured to monopolize the Marchesa's attention as before. She, however, snubbed him most decidedly; though this did not appear to concern him much, for he took chocolate bonbons from the box that stood near him on a small inlaid table, and munched them contentedly without cessation.

Keith was an old acquaintance of the Marchesa's, and 'in fact I look upon him almost as a brother,' she said, in an explanatory fashion to Dorothy.

The latter sat a little apart, very straight and upright on her chair, taking these speeches literally, and wondering what the Marchesa's age might be: she did not look above thirty, yet Dorothy thought she must be older.

'And so this is your wife. Do you like Venice?' said the Marchesa, in pretty, broken English, dragging out her words with affected hesitation, then suddenly relapsing into rapid Italian or French, volubly addressed to Keith.

'We like Venice much, and we are going to stay for the present,' he said. 'It is all new to my wife; she has never been abroad before.'

'Ah, then indeed you will find much to see. Venice is at its best just now, and you are a bride: the place, the climate, all suit. C'est bien ici l'endroit pour faire l'amour, n'est-ce pas?' she added, with a knowing glance at Keith. 'I hope we shall be great friends Mrs. Chester. If I can be of use—you understand, I know everyone in society here. You will entertain, of course? Oh yes,' seeing Dorothy shook her head, 'you must entertain. Mr. Chester, give *un petit bal* to introduce your wife. The fact is, she herself looks like an old picture. You will delight the Italians, madame; we all rave about beauty here. Yes, yes; you must give a *soirée intime*, and we will organize some dinners *al fresco* at the Lido. We must make haste though, for people will soon begin to leave Venice; some of my friends will be most happy to help you. You like that kind of thing?'

'Very much,' said Dorothy, smiling and showing her pretty teeth—glad that she could enter heartily, at least this once, into her animated hostess's plans for her pleasure.

The Marchesa then discussed some mutual friends with Keith in Italian; and the little man—who had been presented to her as Count Pinsuti, and who continued to stare at her unabashed—dragged his chair a little nearer to that of Dorothy, and offered her a bonbon. She thanked him gracefully, and took one, fearing lest a refusal might seem a breach of good manners.

'Very good, n'est-ce pas?' said the little man, floundering in the attempt to speak English, and screwing up his eyes and his forehead as though these contortions gave him greater facility for pronouncing strange words.

Dorothy nodded absently, and allowed her eyes to range around.

The Marchesa, who seemed omniscient, or

rather mesmerically alive to the condition of her guests' feelings, immediately endeavoured to renew the conversation with Dorothy, appealing to her as to her tastes, her occupations, asking her which pictures she preferred, and what were her favourite haunts?

Dorothy answered truly, that it was all very new to her, and she had really scarcely had time to form an opinion; mentally deciding that if she had, her own private and intimate sensations should certainly not be at the beck and nod of an impertinent Italian Marchesa, who asked questions of simple Englishwomen in order to laugh at their mistakes. Dorothy was convinced that the extreme interest expressed by the lady could not be genuine, and that those large lazy eyes only assumed their apparent admiration.

The Marchesa, indeed, could scarcely repress a smile at the evident joy with which Dorothy, like a child released from a lesson, jumped up as soon as Keith said :

'I fear we must not waste any more of your time.'

'No, indeed,' chimed in his wife, eagerly making her adieus.

The Marchesa accompanied them to the door.

'Come soon, again, pray; I am at home on Thursdays. And don't forget, we shall all expect you to give a party.' Then, in a lower key to Mr. Chester, Dorothy having already stepped over the threshold, 'Je vous félicite, mon cher; votre femme est un ange!'

When the Marchesa had bidden her visitors farewell, she turned interrogatively to the ape-like man.

'Well, what do you think?'

'Pretty, certainly,' he said, still munching a bonbon; 'but *fade* — a regular English miss, without manners, or *aplomb*, or anything.'

'I expect she has no vanity. What an unbecoming shady hat she wore; and yet, notwithstanding, one noticed her good looks. I wonder what induced Mr. Chester to marry her —was it *only* for her looks?' mused the Marchesa, lying back in her chair and tapping her feet impatiently on the floor. 'He had money, liberty, beauty. What does a man like that want with marriage? I suppose he *likes* her —*hein?*'

Again she appealed to the incurious Count, who was far happier sitting by her, writing verses to her beauty, carrying her fan, or her shawl, and generally sunning himself in the light of her smiles and popularity, than in discussing the why and the wherefore of an Englishman's marriage.

'Keith was different when he was here last,' she continued, as if to herself; ' he was more *galant*, more lively. That little pale woman looks as if she had taken all the spirit out of him.'

'I am sure I don't know what you would have. He appears in excellent health, and seemed very happy.'

'Ah! you, Count, are always happy, and so you judge others by yourself. I must find out more about this English couple. They interest me—though the bride, certainly, has not my sympathies. I can forgive a woman for being ugly, but not for being *bête*. I suppose she is jealous, too, as she did not wish to give a party. Probably thinks that handsome husband of hers will flirt. Nothing more likely, I should say, remembering what he used to be. If she begins to be jealous, however, she will make some fine misery for herself. I know what jealousy is—moi qui vous parle.'

'You are not jealous of *me*. I give you no cause,' said the little man piteously.

'You! Bah! You don't count. Non, mon ami—I am not afraid of you.'

'I am very devoted,' he said humbly.

'Oh yes—very devoted!' and she turned away with a laugh. 'I think I shall go out now; there may be a breeze from the sea. You are dull company this afternoon, Count.'

She rose, yawned, smelt at a bunch of crimson roses in a glass on the console— finally walked away with a slow and haughty gait.

The little Count began to whistle softly to himself, as soon as he was alone.

'E bene!' he murmured gently; 'é bene ! she is in a bad temper to-day ; but she cannot do without me. It is those stupid English people that have upset her. Povera mia! But she must come in presently; she will want her shawl, and her fan; and it will be, " Count, where are you ? Count, do make haste, see, I am waiting ; I cannot start till you come." I know it all—and it is very pleasant, when the woman is pretty. Ah, per Bacco ! but she *is* handsome, and almost handsomest when she is in a passion ; but she must not take too much interest in that Englishman—he has an Italian look, too. I wonder how the blonde English girl agrees with him ?'

The Chesters spoke but little on the return

journey. But when they were alone together at eventide, sitting side by side on the big sofa, in the dim twilight among the shadows, Dorothy put her arms round Keith's neck, and leaning on his bosom, she said warmly :

' Oh, my darling, how glad I am I have you ! Is society always like the specimen we had of it this afternoon ? Does everybody stare and look coldly at one, and ask stupid questions, while all the time utterly indifferent to the answer? And must one always talk when one has nothing to say? Oh, dear Keith, I hate the Marchesa—I can't bear her and her ways. Do let us stay at home, and be happy together.'

' Dorothy, we cannot always live alone ; you must overcome this foolish shyness.'

' It is not only shyness. Has the Marchesa a husband ?' she added presently, in a dry tone.

' Oh yes ! a dull pompous man, who cares more for gardening and agriculture than for his wife.'

' And who was the little Count ? How ill-behaved he was !'

' Some great friend. I never met him before. Of course, you know, foreign fashions are different to ours. He was probably her *cavalière servente.*'

'Which means——'

'Well, her admirer—her devoted servant. The arrangement is of no importance ; but it has its conveniences.'

'Keith,' said Dorothy, lifting her face from his shoulder, 'let us talk of something else ; my head aches. I wish there were no such things as Marchesas in the world.'

CHAPTER IV.

A VISITOR.

AFTER the lapse of a few days, the Marchesa paid a visit to Mrs. Chester, who happened to be alone. She came unaccompanied, and was beautifully dressed.

Dorothy's shyness diminished considerably when she found herself receiving company in her own boudoir, with familiar objects around her, and the photographs of her mother and sister, in two little velvet frames, keeping her in countenance on a low table. It was far pleasanter thus, than when she was being trotted out in the presence of the ape-like man, for the edification of the critical Marchesa; yet she still possessed few ideas in common with her visitor, and several awkward halts occurred in the conversation.

'Is that the portrait of your sister?' said the Marchesa, noticing the direction of Dorothy's eyes when they sought strength and encouragement in a friendly face. 'She is very nice-looking. How many sisters have you? Only one? Ah, I never had any! I am a spoilt child;' and the Marchesa leant back and laughed consciously.

Not knowing precisely what answer was expected of her, Dorothy made none; and was at once set down by the Marchesa as *décidément gauche.*

The conversation languished a little after this misadventure; the Marchesa herself found it difficult to talk to women of the type of this English girl, who took everything so seriously, understood none of the light sparkles of society chatter, and was only interested in such subjects as pictures, her husband's doings, and improving books.

The Marchesa confined herself therefore to asking questions.

'Cielo! what a life!' she murmured compassionately, as Dorothy related to her the fashion in which her days had passed at Dronington, and described the style of her amusements. 'And you don't play or sing? Mr. Chester used to be very fond of his violin!'

Dorothy shook her head.

'And you have never been to a dance but that one at Lady Darlington's, in honour of the birth of their baby son? Ah, my dear, I pity you profoundly! I adore dancing. When I was your age, I used to go to a ball every night.'

'Indeed, madame,' interposed Dorothy earnestly, 'I have been very happy. Don't pity me, I beg; and *now*——'

'*Now*, of course, is the period of the *lune de miel* — *lune de désenchantement*, as some people call it; but that does not refer to you. Well, certainly men cannot live on ethereal happiness; they want something a trifle more solid. You must not let your husband become *ennuyé*, remember that.'

Dorothy felt a sudden dull thump in the region of her heart. Words like these, only spoken very differently, had been Lady Darlington's last piece of advice: 'Make him comfortable, keep him in a good temper.' The worldly Italian and the simple-minded English lady were agreed in their opinions. What strange creatures men must be if they required so much humouring!

'Your husband has old friends here,' the Marchesa continued, in her vibrating, oily tones ; 'they will naturally want to see a good deal of him. You will be asked to many parties, and you must give some in return. Your husband adores music too ; I remember of old that he is very artistic. You might, to begin with, organize a lovely *fête de nuit*, now the weather is so warm : the effect of lanterns on the water would be exquisite.'

'Doubtless ; but I assure you I have no wish to give a *fête de. nuit*,' said Dorothy, with a touch of dignified composure. 'I don't think Keith would care for it—especially if he thought the idea of it would be distasteful to me.'

' But, *ma chère enfant*, think, how you yourself would enjoy it ! You told me. you thought the dance at the Darlingtons quite perfect.'

'So it was '—here Dorothy blushed—' but I was a girl ; it was all quite different. I don't think married women should dance—at least, I mean I don't care to dance now.'

' Ah, *la petite prude !*' said the Marchesa, gazing with considerable envy and astonishment at the rosy hue mantling Mrs. Chester's cheeks.

The Marchesa could never manage a blush, even with the best intentions. But she con-

soled herself by reflecting that involuntary
blushing was exceedingly disagreeable.

'Society here is not so strict, except, of
course, in Lent. My confessor would never
think of imposing restraints of that sort upon
me. Priests know very well that women
must have amusements.'

'I am a Protestant,' said Dorothy quickly,
mentally invoking a return of her childish
horror of Popery, and of the bigoted intoler-
ance which had procured for an English
Queen the epithet of 'Bloody Mary.'

'Of course you are, you poor thing,' said
the Marchesa, in a tone of irritating pity.
'Our religion is so comfortable; I wish you
could be converted.'

'You need not hope for that; I am firmly
attached to my own religion.'

Dorothy's heart indeed smote her sorely for
having so soon forgotten the good Vicar's ex-
hortations; and she firmly determined to
seek out an English church without fail for
the following Sunday. After all, in a time of
honeymoon abroad, it was not so *very* surprising if ordinary religious duties were a
trifle neglected.

'We will not argue,' said the Marchesa
coldly. 'It was only interest in you that

made me say I wished you were not a heretic;
and I will have a "novena" said for your con-
version, if you like.'

'Thank you, Marchesa,' said Dorothy,
touched with remorse for her uncharitable
opinions ; 'you are very kind, I am sure.'

The Marchesa yawned a little; she had
prolonged her visit, hoping that Keith would
make his appearance : but she had entirely
exhausted her interest in the bride's uneventful past, and she now longed ardently for
something more exciting to happen. At that
instant le Goui entered with some letters on a
silver salver, which he silently handed to
Dorothy. Her eyes sparkled.

'Letters from England,' she said, with a
little catch of pleased excitement in her voice.

'Ne vous gênez pas, chère madame,' said the
Marchesa, rising. 'I will leave you to the
perusal of no doubt good news from your
mother and your sister, and all the sweet,
poetical reminiscences of your sainte jeunesse.
Ah, c'est beau cependant la jeunesse.'

The Marchesa then departed, with a considerable flutter and rustle of garments, and
Dorothy, sitting down, her letters in her hand,
heaved a sigh of relief.

'What a woman! I shall never like her. I

wish Keith had not such a strangely high
opinion of her importance. I am sure she is
worldly and heartless; and oh! I should not
at all like to be at her mercy. She reminds
me, with all her beauty, of a bird of prey.
She has talons, I am sure, though she hides
them under her soft manner.'

The woman of fashion was as yet a type
unknown to our little heroine. At Dronington
her only experience had been of the quiet
villagers immersed in their petty if absorbing
cares—where such questions as to whether close
pews should be abolished for the introduction of
straw chairs, or the church lighted by oil or
paraffin lamps; or whether a district nurse,
quite as necessary if not as important a
personage as the parish-clerk, should be
appointed; or else the topic of Jane Mason's
departure for America, and the marriage of the
smith's son were discussed. The county folk
were steady-going, respectable families, who
performed, like the swallows, an annual migra-
tion to London, and punctually returned at the
close of the season with a show of new bonnets
and smart dresses, which set the fashions for
humbler folk during the ensuing twelve-
months; magistrates, who attended road-meet-
ings, board-meetings, and punctually trans-

acted all local business; their wives, who
taught in the Sunday-school, laid foundation-
stones of churches, and drove in regularly to
the county ball and flower-show; their sons,
who shot partridges and pheasants, rode to
hounds, wore a red coat at dinner, and gave
the sole tinge of liveliness to the proceedings.
Sometimes the daughters wore eccentric
coiffures, or startling lawn-tennis dresses, while
there existed an archery club which had
designed a costume for its lady members of
green and yellow. Again, some interest was
excited by a certain Miss Dewdrop, the daughter
of a brewer, the belle of the county, who gave
herself airs, and might, people whispered to one
another, even marry a duke; but women of
fashion, women who had nothing to do but to
spend money and give *fêtes*, and walk about
all day idle, attended by young men, and were
answerable to nobody for their opinions or their
conduct—women like these Dorothy had never
seen. She could not help feeling as though
some great mystery of iniquity, some of the
flavour of a forbidden fruit, hung about the
Marchesa, marking her out as different from
others of her sex. How, indeed, could this be
possible, Dorothy further argued, seeing the
Marchesa was so perfectly beautiful, so per-

fectly dressed, so sweet and amiable and feminine, and so much admired and esteemed in the highest society ? Being unable to decide this question to her own satisfaction, Dorothy proceeded to open her letters. The first was from Margaret, written in her bold, scrawly hand, a few lines of which almost filled a sheet.

'DEAR DOROTHY' (it began),
 'I am awfully glad to hear you are all right, and the gondolas and the moonshine sound delightful. I think, however, the difficulty of taking a constitutional must be rather a bore though, after a time. I wonder one does not lose the use of one's legs. I walk a great deal in self-defence, having no carriage. How I should like a pony-cart! Those horrid Miss Dewdrops splashed my clean cotton frock from head to foot yesterday, as they drove by; so horribly vulgar of them! Everyone is just as usual. Mamma and I are very dull in the evenings; she generally sleeps a good bit. Then, after I have strummed and sung a little (by-the-bye, I have some new songs), out I go into the garden, which does smell so sweet, and I walk up and down and think. A nightingale has taken up its abode

in a tree near, and sings every night at the same hour; and that rose we planted last year, Souvenir de Malmaison, is beautiful—a mass of blossom. So you see I am not badly off for the romantic; and when there is a moon, the garden is as pretty as Venice, I am sure, and with a little imagination you can take the choruses of the men going home, rather late and rather drunk, for the songs of the gondoliers.

'But really, Dorothy, I feel more and more every day how shabbily you behaved in marrying before me. I think I shall console myself with the doctor—who has rebuilt his house with a new stucco front, a decoration of red tiles and two miniature bay windows, and is evidently on the look-out for a wife—sooner than be an old maid. To be sure, he drives a very seedy gig and smells of whisky; but anything is better than the dulness here.

'Mrs. Parkinson has got a new *protégé*, a gutter child who is to be trained in the choir, taught by the schoolmaster, and clothed by herself, and is to turn out a prodigy. Her cats are quite well. Mrs. Maynard makes bigger eyes than ever at everyone she meets—man, woman, and child included—and gets more and more acid in her sweet barleysugar fashion.

'"How is dear Dorothy? She is such a favourite of mine—quite perfect to my idea; but wasn't it a mistake for her to have married against her mother's wishes?" is a specimen of something she said the other day, but you know it all by heart.

'The Vicar gave us a splendid sermon on Sunday; it was on behalf of a hospital for sick children, and he really pleaded so eloquently that I actually parted with a shilling which I had kept in my pocket intending to devote it to quite another purpose—for a new bonnet. I felt so sorry afterwards I had acted on impulse, which is always a mistake; for I dare say the hospital will not care for the shilling, and I shall have to go on wearing my old bonnet.

'I do hope you will come back soon. What fun it will be to see you do the great lady; besides, you will be able to take me out into society a little. I suppose you will be a swell in the county; but never forget, my child, that it was I, your elder sister Margaret, who eventually clinched your marriage. You and mamma would have gone on crying and arguing till now. She, poor dear, is quite reconciled, however, now. I overheard her the other day dilating on the charming stay her daughter, Mrs. Chester, was making in Italy, and on the quantity of beautiful things her son-in-law had collected in his palace at Venice. Isn't that lovely? You will find us all open-armed and open-mouthed here, ready to receive the bride. They talk of a reception, triumphal arches—what not! I don't mean to help; it would seem *too* ridiculous.

'What *do* you think? Mr. Coote arrived here unexpectedly the other day. He said he had come about some business of Keith's; can you imagine *what* business? He put up at the inn, and stayed nearly all day with us. Actually dined here. Martha really cooked very well, and I had made some pulled bread, and some sandwiches à la chasseur, very hot and very spicy, which he was good enough to pronounce excellent. He is looking sunburnt. That is all the news. Do they wear flounces or frillings at Venice?

'Your always devoted sister,

'MARGARET STRAIT.'

How the words brought Home again vividly before her eyes, and the real goodness of heart that underlay all Margaret's abrupt and careless

speeches ! She could see it all before her—
those long long evenings when the two sisters
had paced up and down in the narrow garden,
with the twilight deepening around them, the
bats flitting past, swooping so low that the
breeze from their wings almost ruffled the
girls' hair; the scent of the white lilies, standing like straight sentinels in the border; the
honeysuckle on the porch, the trailing sheets
of ghostlike clematis hanging against the wall.
And then their talk, so merry, quick with the
joyous consciousness of youth; their innocent
dreams; Margaret's castles in the air, of opera-
boxes and velvet gowns; and Dorothy's high-
strung vision of herself as a modern Vittoria
Colonna, with a second Michael Angelo for her
lover. Each of the girls had their simple
vanity, each dreamt of a blissful future, each
then was panting to begin the journey of life.
Dorothy, indeed, had now already become
a wayfarer, and progressed some distance; that
happy heedless time had dwindled into the
past; her courtship, her marriage, her honeymoon were over, counted as things that had
been; the dreams were evaporated, and she had
awakened to a life of action. She felt years
older than Margaret now. She would no
longer be contented to dawdle in a garden

and weave a maze of bright fancies. No ! She was ready now to take her place, to play her part on life's dazzling stage.

Dorothy sighed, and turned over the other letters in her lap. They were all for Keith, and amongst them she thought she recognised a crabbed handwriting that was familiar to her, in its quaintness and the number of its careless flourishes.

Keith returned in time for dinner, full of interest and curiosity; he had heard from the porter of the Marchesa's visit, and was eager to learn how Dorothy had comported herself.

'How long did she stay ? did she talk much ?'

' She asked questions, and I answered them to the best of my ability. There are some letters for you on that table.'

'Oh yes; of course, the English post has come in. Did you get on quite well, then? You liked her better to-day, I suppose ?'

' I don't think she would care much for my approbation or my liking; she is not that sort of woman. Won't you read your letters?'

Keith had thrown a passing glance at them as they lay on the table, but continued his walk up and down the room.

'The letters can wait. I think we *might*

give a little party ; it would be a nice way
of introducing you to all the people here, as
the Marchesa suggested.'

'Have you been talking to the Marchesa
then ?' Dorothy's eyes flashed as she spoke.

'No, indeed ; but her opinion is not to be
undervalued.'

'Why does she not give a party herself?
Will not that do just as well ?'

'You shall not have any trouble about it,
I promise you. I will get a list of people
from the Marchesa. Our cook is very good,
and there are excellent confectioners in the
town ; and as for le Goui, he can organize
anything, from a *thé complet* for two, to a
state banquet. You need never be afraid of
him.'

'It seems, then, the only person to be
afraid of is myself—whether I shall behave
properly, not look like a wild beast that has
just been caged, betray country manners, and
disgrace you by eating with my knife !'

'Dorothy, I do not recognise you. What
is the matter ?'

When Keith looked at her in his cold, calm,
high-bred fashion, Dorothy immediately became much ashamed of her ebullition. The
fact was: she had realized the whole thing so

acutely, the manner in which she was to be set aside, and treated like some kind of useless doll, while everyone else toiled and busied themselves. She remembered, as a contrast, how at home the girls had alternately been trained to make bread and cakes ; and how she herself, when kneading her dough, had scores of times propped a German or French book in front of her, and read thus, in order not to lose one valuable moment of study while attending to her household cares. But here, unable to speak Italian, she could not even entertain her own guests, while the butler and the cook were far better acquainted with their duties than herself. She hated, as only a proud woman who loves can hate, the sense of being insufficient to her husband's happiness. In addition, she cordially disliked the Marchesa, and these two reasons combined sufficed to make her irritable and uneasy. But Keith's tone, so cold and pained, yet not angry, recalled her to herself.

'Keith,' she said penitently, 'I will do just what you like ; I was wrong to oppose your wishes. I know that you really want to give me pleasure, and that this thing seems almost a kind of duty—and—and—come here, dear, and tell me you are not displeased!'

'Not displeased—a little disappointed, perhaps. I did not think you could be such a
baby—that just because I am proud of you,
and wish you to make the acquaintance of my
friends, you behave like a silly child.'

'I am so sorry, Keith.' She dared not say
again, 'It is because I hate the Marchesa ;'
but she took his hand, dragged him gently on
to the sofa beside her, and put his fingers to
her lips. 'My master, my love, are you not
my all ? how could I grieve you ?'

Keith played a little absently with her hair,
stroking it down, while he thought : Yes ;
obedience in a wife was very necessary. He
was glad she saw and understood it now.

'I wish you were a little more like other
people,' he said gravely, after a pause.

'Am I not ? I will try to be. You will
teach me.'

'Women should never be remarkable except for their charm and amiability. You are
too fond of solitude.'

'Solitude *à deux* is not solitude.'

'No ; but it is an impossibility. No man
can isolate himself with impunity from the
society of his fellows. We should be certain
to quarrel if we were always together alone.'

'Even though I love you so dearly ?'

'Perhaps for that very reason. We have nearly quarrelled now. I am not one of those who appreciate lovers' quarrels, as they are called. Each quarrel destroys one particle of love, and the last quarrel destroys all.'

'I could never cease to love you, Keith ; you seem a part of myself.'

'If we quarrel you will cease to love me ; let us never quarrel.'

'Never, never!' she said fervently, a tear slowly gathering in her eyes and falling upon her pale blue dress.

'There—now you are staining your gown. Don't cry, darling.'

He took her in his arms and kissed her. She put her lips to his, and clung to him like a child that has been chidden ; and thus she shed the first tears of her married life. Where in the whole wide world was she to find comfort now, if *he* turned away from or was cold to her? She had not behaved like Vittoria Colonna to-day, and her Michael Angelo, when grieved, was not one to sit patiently down and write pathetic sonnets. And yet it was a kind of instinct of love that had made her imperatively revolt from submission to the Marchesa's influence—an influence which she felt unconsciously to be baneful, and which seemed, she knew not how, to threaten the confidence that existed between herself and her husband.

A sadness as of impending evil weighed down her spirits ; yet it felt sweet to be encircled in the arms of him who was dearest to her in the whole world—him whom she had cheerfully followed into a mysterious future—him without whom she could not, so she believed now, exist a single day.

Presently Keith loosed her from his arms, and immediately she felt as though a great peace and support had forsaken her. He took up his letters, and broke their seals indifferently.

'Ah,' he said, as he opened the one with the crabbed handwriting, already noticed by Dorothy, 'a letter from Palis—why, the postmark is Milan! He is on his way here. Bravo! he will be in time to help us with our party. He says we may expect him any day. He must never see you cry, Dorothy, or he will think I ill-treat you. Poor old fellow! I am glad he is coming.'

'And so am I ; I took a great fancy to his honest round face, and we got on very well. He wrote some verses for me. You see, Keith, I do like some of your friends ; I like

Mr. Coote, too. By the way, he has been to see Margaret; they were delighted with his visit.'

'It would be a famous marriage for her; Coote is exceedingly well off.'

'Yes, that would indeed be nice,' said Dorothy, by a great effort speaking cheerfully, and wiping away the last of her tears.

CHAPTER V.

PALIS.

PALIS arrived in the very midst of the arrangements for the ball, which from a vague idea had developed into a clear conception, from a conception into an actual fact, and now loomed in all its reality in the shape of piles of invitation-cards, 'menus' on approval, *frotteurs* busily engaged in rubbing parquet floors—one and all scattered variously about the apartments, which were pervaded by a universal smell of wax-candles, turpentine and flowers.

To most people it would have seemed irksome to find themselves among the bustle of preparations such as these; they would have experienced discomfort, reticence, or perturbation; but to Palis the element of agreeable and frivolous activity was precisely delightful.

He gave Dorothy puzzling and comic advice respecting the invitations, designed arabesques and illustrations for the bills of fare, and passed long hours consulting with the cook in the kitchen, licking his lips like a cat before a saucer of milk while discussing the respective merits of celebrated dishes, and with gloating attention superintending the progress of various succulent sauces, into some of which he persuaded the *chef* dexterously to insert a minute flavour of garlic.

'The cuisine of my mother-country,' he would say on these occasions, ' containing the rich Provençal odours which are wafted to my nostrils, and quicken my senses with the memory of past delights, is stimulating, vivifying, and regenerating. Your flabby pale Parisian messes have no savour and no vigour; they are only suited for the palates of *petits crevés*, or of feeble invalids.'

The cook, with sleeves upturned, and a serious importance of mien such as befitted the reputation he was required to live up to, smiled condescendingly at Palis's raptures, and stirred his saucepans with a conscious sense of merit in the presence of so appreciative an admirer.

Occasionally Palis would coax out of him

some delicate dish of shell-fish for breakfast, or
else a concoction of chicken with a remarkably
distinctive flavour ; and of these the ardent
epicure was usually permitted to partake
alone, Keith being too sensitively dainty, and
Dorothy too exclusively British, to share his
tastes. Palis, at least, had thus nothing left
to desire. Gastronomic pleasures, agreeable
society, lavish sunshine, music, and sweet
odours, presented themselves to him in cease-
less variety. He held culinary discussions in
the kitchen, literary arguments in the drawing-
room, and sang out of healthy lungs, to his
heart's content, every barcarolle and chanson
of his repertoire for the delectation of Dorothy,
who, never weary, listened approvingly as she
lounged among her cushions in the gondola.

She also enjoyed amazingly the summer evenings on the lagune, when Palis would bid the
gondolier rest on his oars, and with his rich
sympathetic voice stir the echoes to music.
She would then shut her eyes, and dream away
in a kind of mystic ecstasy ; or else, in a more
critical and artistic mood, watch the pearly
tints of receding buildings, the sheets of gold
upon the quivering waters, the gradual and
tender fading of the rosy clouds into saffron,
opal and cream, until Night drew her pale

curtain, and wrapped all things in the dim loveliness of shadow.

Palis was her usual escort on these occasions, because Keith seemed perpetually engaged. Sometimes it was an old acquaintance who had just arrived in Venice, and who must be visited—sometimes the Marchesa wished to try over some new music with him, or hold an important conference about invitations, or impart to him some new and brilliant idea with regard to appropriate floral decorations— sometimes he must scour the bric-à-brac shops for an ancient ornament, suddenly supposed to be of vital importance—sometimes there were letters to write, lists to make out; but always it seemed imperative for him to leave Dorothy. She felt completely thrust out of his life ; and had it not been for Palis's ever bright society must have been sad indeed.

The Marchesa entirely monopolized Keith's time with music and talk, and engrossed his attention with her own affairs, putting forward the specious plea of Dorothy's inexperience, and her want of knowledge of Italian life and usages, etc.

The implied reproach stung Mrs. Chester keenly; yet she could not but acknowledge its justice, while comforting herself by the assur-

ance that once the ball and its attendant vexa-
tions were past, all would be well, and she
might then employ the amount of wasted leisure
that hung heavy on her hands in a complete
subservience and dedication to her husband's
interests.

'Surely,' she thought, 'ignorance is only a
fault of youth. He knew I was an unpractised
girl—he loved me best so, he said; and I am
not a bit changed. I am willing—oh, so
willing to learn; anxious to be taught; waiting for my master; longing for the day and
hour when I can be his constant companion,
his trusted help-mate, his valuable counsellor.
I have given him my whole life: my sole
wish is for his happiness, and with youth and
strength to aid me, and the willing energy of
love, I cannot fail—I must succeed.'

But her very eagerness to serve, and the
vexation she experienced at her inability,
threw a faint shadow over her lovely face, and
marked her fair brow with a troubled expression. Palis, whose essential quality was
observation—the very bread of a journalist,
according to his own dictum—noticed this; and
with the good-nature he ever displayed when
its exhibition cost him nothing, rallied her on
her want of spirit.

'Why are you sad?' he asked one day, while the gondola floated slowly over the still waters; 'you have everything to make you happy. Are you home-sick?'

'How could I be anything else but happy?' she answered evasively, dipping her hands in the cool sea, and letting the glistening drops trickle one by one from the tips of her fingers. 'I should be an idiot if I were not happy. Have I not everything I could wish for, and a husband who loves me?'

'He does indeed!' said Palis with interest, kindly looking at her; 'but you cannot deceive *me!* There is something which you are trying to hide from everyone, and which frets you. You think of it while your eyes are watching the tints of the sky or sea—you think of it when you lie awake on your bed at night; and for want of telling it to some one you are letting it gnaw at your heart, and take away your appetite. You eat none of those eggs "à la pointe d'asperge" this morning, which Keith and I pronounced excellent.'

'I don't care for eating, as you do,' she said, smiling; 'at least, I am no connoisseur.'

'There you certainly lose a great deal, and reveal a fault of your nature. But you have a graver fault than that—you are morbid.

Why not throw off your feelings, if they depress you, in an article, as I do; or in a poem, like Goethe; or in a picture, like a painter. Nothing destroys beauty like self-tormenting, and beauty is a very precious gift of the gods, not to be lightly despised.'

'Beauty is of no avail if one is otherwise stupid and awkward.' Here Dorothy modestly averted her face.

'You are, excuse me, entirely mistaken. Beauty, to Keith for instance, is the sole desideratum. Look beautiful, fascinate, dazzle everybody at the ball, and you will see and can judge for yourself of the result.'

'I wish I were wiser,' she said, sighing.

'You are quite wise enough, but you are too self-distrustful. Humility never succeeds in society. Look at me. I know my own worth exactly, to a tittle. I have appraised it carefully; I could lend money on it, and not lose a penny. I don't overrate or underrate my value, but you don't suppose I am *quite* such a fool as to inform the world of what it is. I began life as a nobody, without recommendations, powerful protection, or money. But I had plenty of self-possession and a great capacity for work; all I wanted was for the public to give me a hearing. The question was how to obtain it. We all wish and sigh, but we do not all go the best way to obtain our wishes. I waited a little till I could see my chance of a literary career, then I published a book of poems at my own expense; the poems were crude, but they were fresh—full of the impalpable essence of youth, which is strong from its very volatility, like the sparkle of champagne, which infuses a sense of bounding life no dry and matured port wine can give. No one read my poems. " Well, well," said I, " my friends, we'll try again, if you please, and have better luck next time." I struggled to obtain an interview with a great man, a power in the literary world. Impossible; he was always engaged. Naturally I knew it must be so, for I was only a poor devil, and when were poor devils patronized by rich and influential autocrats? At last, as my good star would have it, in his very antechamber, when I was turning away rebuffed and disheartened for the twentieth time, I met a friend. " You don't know Sopwirth?" he said. " All right; come with me." By his side I was of course promptly admitted. I got my chance of speaking to the great man; that was all I wanted. " Young fellow," he was pleased to remark, after we had conversed

a little, " you may be useful to me ; you seem
to have your wits about you. Call again to-
morrow." I called again on the morrow, and
in a week I became his secretary. One day a
leading article had to be written, while he
chanced to be writhing in bed with the gout.
" Let *me* do it, sir," I said quietly, seeing his
sour grimaces. " You ! *could* you do it ?"
" I will try, sir." The article was written
and pronounced a success ; five editions of the
paper sold out that day. Since then I have
lived in clover. I write what I like, go where
I like, and wield a powerful weapon in my
pen. People are civil to me wherever I am.
What has it all to do with you, you ask.
Just this—if I had been humble I should not
occupy my present position. I have always
asserted my own claims, and, consequently,
have always received brevet rank. No one
loves ease better than I do, but no one knows
better how to dispense with it. Here, for instance, I eat and drink and talk to you. Of
course I am come on a special mission ; a
certain amount of copy has to be written—
and it will be written ; a Review started—we
mean it to be a success. But that is no reason
why I should not snap up every scrap of
pleasure that I can attain into the bargain.

Life gives us success, but we must make our own happiness.'

Here Palis leant back, and puffed complacently at his cigarette.

'Happiness depends, surely, more on others than on ourselves. We cannot live alone.'

'Precisely there you mistake. Go to your looking-glass and examine yourself; then array yourself bravely, smile and be happy, and the world is at your feet.'

'Dress would not satisfy me, and *my* world consists of one person.'

'Dress would not satisfy you, but success will. Dress is the means; a smile is your counsellor; success means to you—love.'

Dorothy reddened. Palis discreetly turned away. Perhaps it was only the reflection of the sunset on her cheek. He relit his cigarette, thinking: 'I am wasting my pains; she is only an insipid blonde, as I believed. A nice little woman enough, fit to sit by the fireside and look at her husband with a pair of fond blue eyes, as he yawns in his chair, but no match for a successor of the Borgias.'

Under this fanciful title it was to be surmised that he intended to designate the Marchesa. He certainly admired Dorothy's purely classic beauty, and he was moderately sorry for her *peines de cœur*, if she had any; yet in his heart he almost despised her. The women he loved, perhaps from his own almost feminine intensity of sensation and his habit of referring to himself as an 'old aunt,' were masterful and demonstrative, loud and passionate in their love as in their anger; women of the south, brimful of emotion, and burning with violent sensibility.

Dorothy's very gentleness, her quiet concentration of feeling, seemed to him weakness. He wished to help her, but it was as one helps a snail or worm, by taking it carefully out of the garden-path and placing it on the grass, lest some heedless foot should crush and kill it. In his own prosperous happy career he could afford to do little kindnesses of this sort, warn or advise silly foolish creatures, and be glad of the opportunity.

Dorothy, after this conversation, appreciated him better than she had ever done before. She had always considered him as a delightful companion; now she believed him to have a good heart, and her inclination to like him received a powerful impetus. They spoke no more of sad subjects that day; their talk became bright and merry. Palis related his

experiences of travel in Italy, and kept her
constantly laughing until they returned to the
palace. Some of his advice bore fruit, however. No sooner was Dorothy at home than
she proceeded to her bedroom to consult with
Trimmer about her dress for the ball. She
had not bestowed a thought on it hitherto,
but she now conscientiously endeavoured carefully to weigh the maid's advice. The latter
was addicted to somewhat pompous language,
and had her own ideas of what great ladies
should wear.

'Your dresses are too simple, ma'am,' she
said, 'but I prefer you in blue; this seems to
be the best dress for the occasion, and you
can wear your turquoise and diamond tiara
and ornaments.'

As she spoke she displayed a pale blue
diaphanous dress, decorated with silver braid
and lace.

'Yes, that will do, Trimmer,' said Dorothy,
looking attentively at the dress, while her
thoughts wandered.

'It wants a belt, ma'am; this sash is a
poor thing, and the sleeves are large. I will
nip them in the ghost of a piece, if you like.
When I lived with Lady Mandrake, she would
say to me, "Trimmer, I don't like large

sleeves, they are so vulgar." She was a particular lady, was Lady Mandrake.'

Dorothy had heard stories about this lady already often, for while Trimmer brushed out her mistress's hair, her tongue wagged irrepressibly; and spite of half-hearted interest, Dorothy had become aware of Lady Mandrake's predilections, of the number of powdered footmen she kept, of her French cook, and the early luncheons at which her ladyship gorged herself, permitting her unfortunate daughter and lady-companion only the Spartan supper of dry toast and baked apples, in which her own soul delighted; she knew now by heart about the early drives in the close, yellow-lined coach, and of how the companion and daughter were sent for a *tête-à-tête* drive when they had quarrelled, while Lady Mandrake sat at home to receive visitors, chuckling at her own cleverness, and looking, in her green satin gown and glistening headgear, like some old Indian idol before its worshippers. Lady Mandrake never fell out with Trimmer, who alone understood her ways and the mysteries of cosmetics, hair-dyes, and an abstrusely complicated toilet. As Trimmer cheerfully remarked, ' Had it not been for her ladyship's premature demise after a large luncheon-party,

I should never have been at liberty to take another situation.' Lady Mandrake left her faithful servant a legacy of ten pounds to buy mourning with, and a first-rate character, besides a wealth of stories and anecdotes with which to enliven her succeeding employers ; but Dorothy was very weary of the stories and sayings, and of Lady Mandrake's ill-natured behaviour to her dependents ; especially was she weary to-day when, sitting on a high velvet chair, she contemplated her blue draperies, and listened to the maid's complacent remarks.

'Does it want a band?' she said innocently; 'then make one.'

Trimmer looked aghast. Lady Mandrake had nothing made at home, for all her dresses came from Paris; so she stood there like a statue of surprise, petrified by fear, one finger continuing to point to the extended folds of the dress, while Dorothy wearily rested her head on her hand. Suddenly Keith made an irruption into the room.

'Looking at your dresses, Dorothy, I perceive. Are you very busy?'

'Not in the least, dear,' said she, rising with alacrity and twining her arm into his.

'I was just remarking that this dress requires a band, sir,' said Trimmer severely.

'Is that your ball-dress? It will suit you beautifully. Wants a band, does it? Well now, how fortunate! I remember I saw in a shop the very thing—an old silver belt set with large turquoises. I will buy it at once.'

'No, no! pray don't, Keith. Trimmer is mistaken; I do not require it.'

'Yes, you shall have it; it is a fine thing in itself, and will certainly complete your toilette. The man is a dreadful Jew, but I can get it, I think, for little above its real value.'

Trimmer smiled to herself as she refolded and put away the dress. 'Mr. Chester was a perfect gentleman, surely; but as for his wife, well, it was evident enough that, with all her beauty, she had not mixed much in good society,' was the comment of the sagacious maid.

CHAPTER VI.

AT A BALL.

A HUM of voices pervaded the palace, whose sumptuous galleries and reception-rooms were flooded with light from the rays of thousands of candles. The large gilt doors were thrown back to their widest extent; a gay throng of women, whose bare shoulders and glancing jewels gleamed from the multitudinous mass of silks and satins, the men making hideous black patches in the luxuriance of colour, streamed up the marble staircase, which was half hidden by banks of tropical and sweet-scented plants and flowers. Within the entrance of the grand gallery Dorothy, in her blue dress, stood, calm and self-possessed, by the side of her husband, holding in her hand a bouquet of white roses, and pleasantly receiving her company. There was something so pure and so noble in her simple, gracious fashion of welcome, that it converted the universal curiosity into universal respect and admiration. Palis, from his vantage-post behind a marble console, could hear the remarks of the company and notice the impression she created. At first there was some surprise expressed at the simplicity of her dress—the blue cashmere falling in numerous straight folds, and being gathered in at the waist like that of a Greek statue; her hair rippling in pretty natural waves, tightly coiled and crowned by the tiara of turquoises and diamonds; the antique silver belt encircling her slim waist. She wore neither a necklace nor a bracelet. Some of the women cavilled.

'She is full of pretensions, and tries to do the *ingénue*, that is clear,' said one recognised beauty to the other.

The men raved of her extreme fairness, and the dark Italian ladies threw angry glances at their attendant swains.

'She will do,' thought Palis to himself, as he walked towards one of the open windows, whose balcony had been converted into a bed of roses. 'She has excited admiration and envy—the two conditions of success—and she seems quite unconscious of it all. Keith must be gratified.'

Keith, indeed, seemed to be gratified; for the company having ceased to arrive, he left the post of reception, and danced and talked, and found seats for the old ladies, making himself generally agreeable.

Dorothy had refused all invitations to dance, and stood leaning silent and abstracted against the large gilt doors, fingering the roses in her bouquet. She was tired of smiling and bowing and shaking hands; and as everyone was engaged, she could afford herself the luxury of silence for a few moments.

The ape-like Count stood at her side, but he did not speak. He was watching the Marchesa —a magnificent apparition in a crimson robe. She and Keith were waltzing; the latter cheerfully nodded to his wife as he passed by, and after a few turns, stopped with his partner at the far end of the ball-room.

The Marchesa was speaking eagerly. He listened and looked grave. Her beauty had never showed to greater advantage; the pale ivory of her skin contrasted finely with the colour of her dress; her lips were ruby-red; her eyes vied in brightness with the diamonds in her jetty hair.

'The Marchesa Bellaggio looks well to-night,' one man said to another, close to Palis's elbow.

'Splendid! She understands dress. I think Chester is of our opinion. He gazes into her eyes oftener than he need.'

'Bah! He's just married. What is your impression of his wife? C'est une grue, je pense. Une petite poupée, pâlie par les brumes d'Angleterre. For myself, I prefer more colour.'

'So do I, as a rule ; but that rose-leaf complexion is very pretty. She is a contrast to the other women.

'I like her style of Marguerite dress : the simple hair, the girdle. What will you bet that those are all studied effects ?'

'They say she is quite a country girl he picked up in a village, and that he has asked the Marchesa Bellaggio to give her some lessons in " chic."'

'She may teach her some other lessons, if he does not take care. I wonder if the petite femme is jealous ?'

'Apparently she is not. The Marchesa arranged the whole affair of the ball, decided who was to be invited, etc.; while Mrs. Chester was doing the platonic with that fellow Palis, the journalist.'

'Sapristi!' muttered Palis to himself, 'I had better get out of this, or I may hear something which will necessitate my quarrelling with one of those fine gentlemen; and that is an item which was not included in Keith's programme, and which he might not like. What brutes those fellows are! I will go and talk to Mrs. Chester; she looks somewhat triste.'

Dorothy's eyes sparkled when she beheld Palis. His kind open face seemed so familiar and welcome, whereas the sea of unknown countenances around had caused her an impression of solitude.

'Will you take a little turn with me?' he said. 'I see there is a lull in your duties, and an ice will refresh you. Let us go this way; there is less of a crowd.'

'Why do you not dance?' she asked, as he gave her his arm. 'You are so foreign in your tastes, I am sure you must love dancing.'

'I did, but I fear I have a little lost my figure; though it is plain enough to see that I had lessons of deportment in my youth.' Palis spoke in a bantering tone, and looked ruefully at the decided obesity of his lower man. 'A sedentary life ruins one's figure,

but after all it is the countenance that matters
—not the waist.'

' I am afraid I managed very badly to-night,'
Dorothy said, when she received her ice, as
they stood near the window looking out upon
the silvered waters. ' Those Italians speak
so fast—and I cannot even understand their
French, much less their Italian ; but I tried
to remember what you had said about not
being humble.'

' You appeared very self-possessed,' said
Palis, nibbling at a large slice of chocolate-
cake he had secured for himself. ' You will
soon get into the way of these things, and
when once you learn to know their monotony,
you will have forgotten to be shy. What do
you think of society ?'

' It seems rather a waste of time. Dancing,
of course, is pleasant enough ; but in a crowd
there is not much conversation possible, and
at the best it is very desultory.'

' People don't come into society for improving conversation ; but it is most amusing to
watch all the little tricks and jealousies. I
am never tired of it. Society means, you know,
the art of outshining one's neighbours; wearing bigger diamonds than one's acquaintances
who wear little ones, or can only afford paste ;

driving a carriage-and-pair when one's friends
are forced to be contented with a fiacre ; and
asking more people, and spending more money,
burning more candles, and wasting more flowers
than anyone else.   Such is society, and therein
consists the delight of it.   The gratification of
vanity is far more consoling than the enjoy-
ment of mere pleasure.   Anyone can have that
—a ride in the country will give it, or a quiet
picnic ; a daisy will do as well as a tulip ; a
violet as well as a gardenia ; a cloud as well
as a gown of poult-de-soie—but then it affords
no scope for vanity.   You perceive ?'

' What a dreadful view of human nature !'

' Society is an aggregate of all human
vices; there is no room for the virtues.   If
you do as I do—find your recreation in
laughing at them—you will never be dull.'

' That would be hateful to me.'

' Not really.   Do you see that little woman
there in pink ?   She is as ugly as sin, but a
most successful flirt.   Her tongue is as sharp as
a needle ; and she amuses everyone.   She has
lots of admirers, plenty of adulation, and not a
single friend.   The man with her has a pretty
wife, whom he leaves at home to cry her eyes
out, because she is stupid, and cannot make
his house lively.   Probably she will console
herself in time ; at present, she sheds tears,

and thus drives her husband still farther away.
Men cannot bear inundations of salt water.
One never sees her without red eyes in public;
and, after all, how can one love a woman with
red eyes?   Leah certainly had them, but then
it was her misfortune, not her fault ; and I
dare say, though Jacob behaved exceptionally
well to her, she had to suffer many " mauvais
moments " from Rachel's caprices.   But I see
you are not listening, Mrs. Chester ; shall we
go back to the ball-room?"

Dorothy's observant eyes had noticed Keith
disappearing through a door with the Marchesa on his arm ; she thought he looked exceptionally radiant.   It was not surprising
that, in his own house, with so handsome a
woman by his side, and adulation and compliments surrounding him, he should seem
happy ; and yet such is the contradiction of
human nature, that Dorothy involuntarily
wished he had not looked so happy.

Presently Palis left her, and she remained
standing alone under a candelabra, till she
was joined by several young men, who
hastened to pay their court to her.   The light
from the candles threw a pale transparency
over her features, and outlined her fair head,
with its circlet of diamonds, against the dark

satin background. There was something very pathetic and charming in her appearance, and Keith, happening to be free at the moment, glanced in her direction, and caught sight of her graceful figure.

'I have never valsed with my wife,' he thought; and a thrill of conjugal pride passed through his heart. 'Dorothy, will you valse with me?'

At the sound of his voice, the crowd of empty admirers melted away on each side, and the two were left alone. The number of dancers had diminished ; some were enjoying the fresh air on balconies ; some flirting in the ante-room, which was filled up like a tropic greenhouse with palms, and ferns, and fountains ; some were eating ices in the tea-room. The parquet floor looked invitingly smooth and cheering ; the orchestra was playing a ravishing valse.

'Come,' urged Keith, 'you have not danced yet !'

'I don't know if I can dance.'

She hesitated, and thought with longing that it would be sweet to twirl to such strains in his arms.

'Every girl can valse. I am sure you are as light as a feather. Come !'

Almost before she could answer, he had his arm round her waist, and they had glided off over the slippery floor.

Keith danced beautifully; it had been one of his principal accomplishments when, as a diplomat, he had led most of the cotillons at Rome. His arm guided his partner firmly, and his steadiness supported her. But Dorothy, fluttered with happiness, and unaccustomed to the exercise, turned giddy after a few paces, staggered, and would have fallen, had he not held her upright, and presently pushed her into a chair.

'Are you better? Why, you look quite pale!' he said, anxiously examining her face. 'Dorothy, what was it?'

'I don't know; I so seldom dance. And now—oh dear!—I have lost all the rest of that turn; and the music is delightful.'

'Yes, it is a good swinging tune; but you had better stay here. I will fetch you a glass of water.'

An elderly lady, owning a pair of very yellow shoulders, and sparkling with diamonds, now proffered her large black fan, and stood sympathizingly over her, talking volubly, and addressing her remarks to the by-standers.

'Poor thing! the heat of the room and the

dancing have been too much for her. Her husband seemed so concerned — quite in a dreadful way ; but I dare say she will soon be better.'

The flow of words fell like the sound of rushing waters upon Dorothy's ears ; and a bitter thought, bearing the sting of a serpent, pierced her to the heart. She had again disappointed Keith. *What* must he think of her —he, who hated fuss? How stupid it was not to be able even to dance without turning giddy! Keith presently appeared with the water; but the old lady, who turned out to be a personage of importance, still talked on. Dorothy thanked him with a loving look. And now the Marchesa approached.

'Madame is ill ! Ah, you had better stay quietly near the open window, there—the fresh air will soon revive you! Mr. Chester,' she added unconcernedly, ' *what* time is supper ? And you really must explain to me how that figure of the masks in the cotillon should be performed.'

They disappeared together ; and Dorothy, now forsaken by the old lady, who had gone off on the arm of an elderly admirer in search of refreshments, remained alone, somewhat sad and chilly. She was not permitted the

respite long, however; for, supper being announced, Count Pinsuti claimed her, and kept
her attention constantly occupied in efforts to
understand his barbarous French.

Palis sat on her other hand, pleasantly
busy with pickled cucumber and a salad of
crabs. At the far end, among a glitter of plates
and flowers, sat enthroned the Marchesa and
her host, at whom she threw killing glances
from her languorous black eyes, and smiles
from a row of pearly teeth. She had a fashion
of appearing absorbed in the person who was
her companion for the moment, usually thought
specially attractive; and on this night she
chose to be absorbed in Keith.

'Will you dance the cotillon?' he asked,
heaping her plate with strawberries.

The intimacy between them had surprisingly
increased.

'I am not sure if I shall dance;' she tossed
her head.

'Will you dance with me?'

'Do you mean it, or is it only the civility
of mine host? I don't require any humbug
from you, for you know you are a married
man now!'

'Yes.'

Keith looked, and her bright orbs flashed

also at the moment in the same direction, to
where Dorothy presided composedly, looking
pure and ethereal.

'Mr. Palis seems very devoted. Is he an
old friend of your wife's?'

'He is *my* friend!' said Keith, with intention.

'Ah!'—the lady's 'ah!' was expressive—
'she is very lovely; no wonder he likes to sit
beside her!'

'I fancy the supper is a greater attraction
than my wife,' Keith said, laughing. 'Palis
is a gourmet.'

'I thought he was only a journalist. Does
literature pay, then, in England?'

'Palis contrives to make it do so; but his
tastes are simple, and his rooms only a front
and back drawing-room, in which the tables are
strewed with papers.'

'Horrid!' She made a pretty little *moue.*
'I know—dirt and cobwebs, a grubby dressing-
gown, and a greasy breakfast-set, and the maid-
of-all-work in curl-papers. I have read of such
things.'

'No, no; it is not so bad as that. We
have had some pleasant literary breakfasts
together, old blue crockery on the table
garnished with a bowl of gold-fish, a water-

lily floating in the middle; good company and good talk, and first-class omelettes.'

'I have finished; shall we go?' she said, indolently making a movement to rise.

'And the cotillon—you will dance it with me?'

'Perhaps; if you deserve it.'

How different are the meanings of words according to the sense in which they are intended, and the person by whom they are used! A soldier deserves the Victoria Cross—that is, valour; a sister of mercy deserves a heavenly crown—that is, self-immolation; a poor person deserves relief—that is, poverty; a diplomat deserves the blue ribbon—that is, astuteness, perhaps also a little falsehood; a young man deserves a reward at the hands of his lady—that is love sometimes, generally flattery.

Keith took care to deserve the lady's hand for the cotillon when the moment arrived. Chairs were being ranged round the room, strange-looking banners, waving ribbons, gaunt sticks, ungainly masks, tambourines, and large baskets of sweet-smelling flowers, were being brought in by watchful attendants and disposed about. The orchestra, well refreshed—the leader a trifle flushed with good wine, his acolytes pale and haggard with many nights' watching of the happy disportings of others— took their places, tuned their instruments, and began the inspiring valse.

'I suppose we had better go,' said a British matron to her plain daughter; 'these things are interminable, and you have not got a partner. What is the use of staying to see a parcel of foreigners dance?'

'Oh, mamma, pray stay! I may have a partner presently; and I hear the presents are going to be lovely.'

The speaker had thin red arms, and an eager face, and it was her first season. The fond mother forthwith relented, and the two women stood for the remainder of the evening against the door, watching, carping, and cavilling.

'Mrs. Chester does not dance,' remarked a young attaché to his friend.

'No; it's a pity. She's awfully handsome, and nice to talk to; doesn't snap a fellow up a bit. But, I say, Chester *is* carrying on to-night!'

'Oh, he always does! I declare, that pretty little Fairfax girl has no partner, I must go and ask her.'

They were all settled now : the couples sat in a circle, like a wreath of flowers with their colours mingled; the elderly diplomats, husbands, or fathers, loitering about in little knots, twirling their moustachios, and talking scandal or politics.

Dorothy, having attended to her guests, now took refuge behind a curtain, and breathed the fresh air from the window. No one had noticed her disappearance, and she could safely look out into the quiet night, murmurous with the sound of lapping waters and the distant cries of the gondoliers. The morning was breaking ; fleecy grey clouds were rising on the horizon, the pallor of day mixed with the azure of moonlight ; pigeons cooed softly. Behind her was the room with its lights, and its intoxicating rhythmic music, and the warm breath of flowers, and the heated luminous atmosphere. She could see, by half turning, Keith and the Marchesa floating round contentedly in the mazes of the dance. How lightly she moved, how easily he held her! She could catch fragments of their talk. Ah! why had she herself behaved so stupidly? What must Keith think of her now? Out there on the canal it was so peaceful and quiet. The smell of the sea seemed to carry a freshness with it—a health, a reality, in which the visions of the ball-room were wanting.

She moved a little forward, and leant looking in among the dancers. They were dancing the flower-figure: Keith stood in the middle, guiding and directing people, occasionally gaily clapping his hands. Dorothy's pale face, peering from the curtains, arrested his attention. He had a bunch of red carnations in his hand ; and he immediately hastened up and presented them to her.

' You ought to take a turn with me for them,' he said ; ' but I will excuse you, since dancing makes you giddy. Are not these carnations sweet ? Don't overtire yourself, darling.'

Before she could speak he had glided off again. The Marchesa's sharp eyes had seen the whole of this little episode. When he rejoined her where she sat, her bodice pinned all over with the bouquets presented by her friends, she said in a cold sarcastic tone :

' Bravo, mon cher ! bien, très bien ! You are a man of the world, you neglect nothing. I liked your little domestic idyl. Carnations mean devoted love ; I only gave you a yellow rose, that means jealousy. I am sorry the ball is nearly over; it has been a dream of beauty. Let us appreciate the present, at least; let us try to prolong it.'

'A man has always a past and a present,' he said sadly.

'And a future. *You* have forgotten the past!'

'I never forget the past; at least, not some things.'

'Shall you forget to-night ? I do not want you to forget it.'

'There are some moments one can never forget,' he said absently.

He took the yellow rose, as he spoke, from his button-hole, and hid it in his breast-pocket.

'No, do not forget,' she whispered with a bewitching look, rising to dance again. Dorothy had not heard the words, but she had seen Keith's action. The ball seemed to her suddenly like the dance of death, figures whirling furiously into a mad vortex; the hurrying tones of music, the noise, the heat, the late hour, the breaking morning striving with its cold grey rays to drown the glare of candles, impressed her like some hideous phantasmagoria ; the men became satyrs, the women bacchantes ; a skull seemed to peer from beneath circlets of jewels, death's heads to gibber under flowery wreaths; the dancing, the movement, the scents, turned her giddy and faint. As in a horrible nightmare, the garish scene oppressed her till she almost gasped for breath. At that instant a pale streak showed above the horizon; it widened and grew redder; it turned to gold, and tipped the domes and steeples; it glittered on the roofs, it made the heavens all a blaze. The sun had risen. She turned her back upon the sight and sounds of revelry, and stepped out on to the balcony. She gripped the cold stone with her hot hand, while the breeze cooled her feverish cheeks. She ceased to hear the music, which, indeed, had stopped; a perfect peace lulled her senses, and her heart no longer throbbed. Away out on the lagune she could see little boats with orange sails calmly floating, while the sky was blue overhead ; then she drew her hand across her eyes, as though to efface from her brain the thoughts of the past night.

' Dorothy, is that you?' said a voice at her elbow suddenly, Keith's calm, languid voice ; ' I thought you had departed long ago to bed, worn out with your exertions. I have seen the last of the guests to their gondolas ; everyone is gone, and I am just off to the Lido to bathe. I don't feel a bit sleepy, and a swim will do me a world of good. Goodnight, darling ; take a rest now at once.'

He kissed her lightly on the forehead and was gone. She could hear him humming the last bars of the cotillon valse as he went down the gallery. For a minute or two she stood motionless, looking after him ; then she also crept slowly and noiselessly away. The servants were already beginning to gather up the fragments of the ball; and le Goui met her, carrying a silver candelabra from the supper table. Her room was full of sunshine, and she was alone and quiet at last. She flung herself down full-dressed on her sofa, for Trimmer had retired hours ago to rest.

CHAPTER VII.

DOROTHY SPEAKS.

THERE sleep must have eventually overtaken her, for when she awoke some hours after, Keith was standing over her, his two hands in his pockets, contemplating her figure as she lay on the sofa, a crumpled mass of drapery around her, and her hair tossed in wanton waves about her brow. She slowly opened her eyes, feeling chilly and aching in every limb, and raised herself with difficulty. Keith's face wore a half-mocking smile.

'Dorothy, what *is* your reason for choosing this extraordinary position to sleep in?'

At this question all her troubles returned to her mind—the Marchesa's serpentine attractiveness, Keith's attentions, the yellow rose he had placed in his breast-pocket, her

own strange wild sensations; finally, the lassitude that had overpowered her.

'Where is the yellow rose?' she said; 'what
did you do with it?'

Keith stared; he had already forgotten.

'What yellow rose?'

'The one the Marchesa gave you, and which
you seemed to prize so dearly.'

'Ah, *that!* Well, I think I lost it when I
went to bathe. Do you want it? and, pray,
where are my carnations?'

'Here!' she pulled some faded flowers from
her bosom.

'That's right; I am glad you kept them.
Now, dear, dress and come to breakfast. I
don't believe any woman but yourself would
risk wearing an evening gown in this broad
daylight after a ball, and still look lovely.
How white your shoulders are! and my poor
tiara, look where it lies!'

The tiara, indeed, had fallen on the floor by
the hem of her gown, and now glimmered
brightly against the thick pile of the Persian
rug.

'Oh, Keith, I am so sorry! I was very
tired, and I fell asleep. And where have you
been? and why do you look so bright while I
feel utterly exhausted?'

She spoke gaily, but Keith noticed that her tone was different, and that she carefully averted her eyes.

'You are overtired; that is all, darling,' he said, stooping down to her and putting his cheek against hers, which was rosy with the glow of her late slumbers. 'Just think how long I have been knocking about, and going to balls and leading cotillons. I am an old war-horse now, well inured to all these things, but *you* are a little country girl. You will feel better after you have had some breakfast. I had a capital swim.'

'Had you?' Dorothy still reclined listlessly on her sofa, fingering the tiara in her lap. 'You must take me with you another time.'

'Certainly; a number of people were out already this morning, and two ladies, the Marchesa Bellaggio and her cousin—capital swimmers.'

'She has been with you already this morning?' Dorothy said, starting to her feet.

'Yes; why not? They decided not to go to bed, like myself, and to take a longer afternoon siesta instead. Why do you look so astonished? Surely,' as the fact slowly dawned upon him, and his wife's deeds and words were revealed to him in a new light—'Surely you are not jealous?'

She did not answer, and her cheeks, which had suddenly paled, now flushed a little.

'Jealous! Dorothy—after all your protestations of love.'

'It is because I love that I may feel jealous,' she responded briefly.

'Bah!' Keith shrugged his shoulders expressively. 'Jealousy is a confession of weakness; but after all, I suppose you are only a woman, like the others.' He turned away with a scowl on his brow.

'Keith, Keith! don't you see'—she caught him by the arm as she spoke—'don't you see that I cannot bear it? You looked at her so strangely; you put her rose in your breast-pocket; you danced so much with her; you went out this morning to meet her.'

'Rubbish! I went to have a swim, to cool myself after the hot rooms.'

'Is it jealousy anxiously to guard the treasure one values? Is it jealousy, having given one's self utterly to a person, to feel as though if his face turned away from one it would mean death? If this is jealousy, Keith, then I am jealous—because I love you!'

'You must be a fool, child, to put all these

sinister meanings into the simplest acts. I
have lost the rose, as I told you. The Marchesa thinks nothing of these trifles : they are
the insignificant courtesies of society; they
make one popular; they pass the time—that
is all ! *You* are my wife ; but that does not
prevent my talking and laughing with other
women—especially when they are clever and
" æsthetic." ' The Marchesa is a wonderful
musician.'

Dorothy was seeking to read his thoughts,
scanning him with her serious, deep eyes ; she
felt puzzled and unsatisfied. He continued :

'Don't look at me like that, as if I had
committed a crime ! The Marchesa is a
pleasant companion, a true artist, a——'

'She is a dangerous woman, I know she
is ! I overheard two men discussing her last
night. They said you had taken the place of
Count Pinsuti ! What did they mean?'

'Only idle talk ; the babble of men who have
nothing to do but to invent scandal about their
neighbours. Italian men have no occupation.'

' Keith, I hate her !'

' I am sorry for it, my dear,' he said composedly. ' You will have a great deal to do
if you begin by hating every woman I speak
to. You have me here always ready by your

side. You see more of me than anyone else does. Is not that enough for you?'

' No, it is not enough!' and her eyes shone tenderly.

' I can't stand jealous women.'

' You have not had a wife before, Keith. I am not a woman only—I am your wife!'

' Listen, Dorothy! I loved a woman once, some years ago, and she turned my life into a hell by her jealousy. Don't you begin it. I could not stand it!'

' She died, did she not?'

' She died,' he responded curtly.

' And shall I die, too? I *can* die for you, Keith. It seems to me as if, under some conditions, dying were easier than living.'

She spoke very quietly, and her look had a far-off serenity.

' You will live to a good old age. You have splendid health, Dorothy.'

' Keith, *you* are my life! Do not deceive me!'

' I haven't a thought of it, my dear!' her tone was too earnest to suit his frame of mind. ' Are you coming to breakfast?'

A break in sentiment generally dispels it.

' Yes, I will come. But, Keith!'—she put her arms round his neck and touched his lips

with hers—' remember I have given you my
life! What should I do with it, if you—cared
for another?'

It gave him a strange kind of sensation
when this loving, pleading woman in the low
dress, with the silver trimmings glinting in
the sunlight, clung to him, her golden dis-
hevelled hair half hanging about her shoulders,
her warm red lips lifted to his, and the sharp
sound of pain in her voice as she talked. He
soothed her as one would a child, pleased
with her beauty, and yet a little wearied with
the chains he had himself riveted, and which
were the cause of her exactions. He kissed her
fondly again and again, not saying much, but
implying everything by his caresses, till she
was calm. That auspicious moment arrived,
he left her to the hands of Trimmer, who now
presented herself, eager to perform her accustomed duties.

' You should have let me sit up for you,
ma'am,' she remarked briskly, while she vigorously brushed out her mistress's hair. 'It is
very injurious to fall asleep by an open window.
No wonder you are chilly! Lady Mandrake
avoided draughts as she would poison ; and
it's my belief it was owing to those precautions
that she survived to a good age.'

'I should not care to live to be very old,' said Dorothy, whom the maid's chatter bored. 'Everyone must die some day.'

'Yes, indeed, ma'am; and it's well to be prepared, as the prayer-book tells us. But premature deaths seem to be more unprepared like. I should like to die comfortably in my bed, with my hair all smooth and tidy, and a frilled bed-gown, if I were a lady.'

Dorothy smiled a little, and cut the conversation short by taking up a book.

Keith, meanwhile, moodily smoked a cigarette in his wife's sitting-room—the only apartment to which normal order had been restored—in company with Palis, who had had a good supper, a good sleep, and was now on the *qui vive* for a good breakfast.

'What's the matter?' said the latter, when he had watched for some minutes the curling rings of smoke from his friend's cigarette. 'You look out of sorts this morning. I always say it is a mistake not to get a night's rest. You young men try perpetual experiments with your health, and then—patapouf! —one morning there comes a fit of the gout, or a neat little paralytic attack, and you are *flanqué* with a real bad illness.'

'Ill-health is a bore, I dare say. I never

experienced it. But, Palis, it is women who are the real difficulty. One never knows how to take them. The gentlest and the best have the secret of tormenting one.'

'A conjugal row?' asked Palis gravely; 'it is early days, surely!'

'No such thing—no one could have a row with Dorothy; it is the extreme sensibility of her nature which frightens me; she feels things so acutely.'

'She looks always very quiet.'

'Still waters run deep, you know. I believe I was a fool to marry,' he added, with a sigh. 'There is too much of the Bohemian in my nature. I am too contradictory.'

'You will get accustomed to it. Harness tames even a racehorse.'

'Jealous, bah!' said Keith, as if to himself. 'Why the dickens should anyone be jealous? If a thing is yours and you value it, keep it; if it isn't, what's the use of fretting?—there are as good fish in the sea as ever came out of it.'

'But that doesn't apply to wives and husbands. Your choice once made, is made for ever.'

'Yes, indeed; as Hume says, "I had my choice of a prison, but that is but a small comfort, since it must still be a prison." We

are all apt to make blunders, and it is a bore
if the blunder be irrevocable.'

' Mrs. Chester looked lovely last night.'

' I know she did. She's lovely—a thousand
times handsomer than the Marchesa of whom
she is jealous, who is at least ten years older,
and uses pearl-powder ; but the Marchesa is
good company, has fine eyes, and amuses me.
One goes into society to be amused.'

' Mrs. Chester doesn't understand that, I
suppose?'

' She doesn't, more's the pity.'

' Did she cry?'

' No, but I saw the tears in her eyes. She's
a darling, and I'm a brute. But I can't help it;
jealousy completely disgusts me. It is a weak
vice. Revenge I can understand—a man might
get some satisfaction from that.'

' Do you know why jealousy annoys you?
Because it gives you trouble—forces you to
take one side or the other, to care for something.
You are a thorough sceptic, Keith.'

' So are you.'

' Pardon, mon cher, I use other men's preju-
dices for my own advantage. I use them
knowing what they are worth; I neither rail
at nor despise them. But, *au fond*, I have my
own ideas. I say the prayers every day which

my mother taught me as a child. I have a respect for my country. I never lie except from necessity. I owe no man anything, and I am true to my friends. I make love to many women, but I take good care not to marry one.'

'The worst of it is, I love my wife dearly, and yet I do the things that make her miserable. Can you account for it? I really do mean to make her happy, only somehow she does not understand it.'

'I imagine a man never really loves a woman that he does not make her suffer more or less for his infatuation. You must sugar the pill, my boy—make up to Mrs. Chester in other ways.'

'Presents! I have it. I'll go out directly and buy her something—money shall be no object. We will go together, you and I, and I will bring back the smile to the eyes that have shed tears. Not but what I suppose it's really as natural to women to cry as it is for men to whistle; it never seems to spoil their complexion or their appetite so long as the exercise is indulged in in moderation.'

The day, which had commenced in golden splendour, now gradually grew cloudy; by the time Keith returned with the filigree earrings he intended as a peace-offering for his wife

the sky was gloomy and overcast, and in the
afternoon rain began to fall heavily. Mr.
Chester and his friend, possessed by the
usual masculine restlessness, sallied off to
play billiards at the Cercle ; and Dorothy
remained alone. Her heart was heavy, and
her head ached; she could settle to no occupation ; the night's dissipation had unstrung
her nerves and fatigued her body. She sat at
the window with a volume of Macaulay's
'Essays' on her lap; but she neither turned the
leaves of her book, nor managed to attune her
mind to reading, and only idly followed with
her eyes the perpendicular falling drops in
their junction with the turbid waters of the
canal. Bright, beautiful Venice had lost her
character to-day; she was dull and grey and
gloomy. The sparse gondolas that crept sadly
along were closed and dingy ; the happy, gaudy
population of the streets had disappeared like
the butterfly before the storm ; the wind sobbed
round the carved balconies of the old Gothic
palace, and echoed the sadness of Dorothy's
heart. Keith's present of the filigree earrings
lay beside her in their velvet-lined morocco
case, but they gave her no pleasure. She instinctively felt that they were bestowed as a species
of bribe.

'I shall never say anything more,' she thought; 'but if he understands me so little, things can never be the same again. To think that earrings could compensate for his not caring for me as much as I thought!'

Mrs. Chester was inexperienced; she had given up her own ambitious dreams for the sake of love, and she forgot that her husband's views on the subject might not comprise equal self-surrender. She forgot that a prize once possessed loses its value proportionately in a man's eyes.

Dorothy verily lived in his house, under his eye, ready to appear at breakfast, dinner, and all reasonable hours; how, therefore, could she expect to be always in his thoughts? It is a very common and early mistake, that of judging other's feelings by our own. True and enlightened sympathy is the gift of advancing years, of increased and bitter experience; it is the heritage of suffering, the price of pain. In youth the tones of the spirit are not finely attuned; they do not vibrate in perfect unison with the emotions of others, nor give out a full and harmonious sound at the touch of our groaning fellow-creatures: the heart is too self-absorbed to know aught but that it lives and loves, and glows and suffers. It is only when that heart has been rudely torn and shaken and trampled upon, when the glamour of pleasure and desire has been rent aside, and the cry of humanity, going up from a thousand lips, seems to find an echo in our aching heart—it is only then that Sympathy can extend her healing touch, and in helping others learns the secret of her own joy.

Keith was worldly and Dorothy was selfish— through the very love which, exalting her idol above heaven, left her defenceless alone on earth—and each exacted from the other that which it was out of either's power to give. Thus it seems to be always in life: we go blundering and stumbling along, like supers on an un- lighted stage, till one day unexpectedly a brilliant stream of light falls on us, illuminat- ing all the dark places, and we see ourselves and others clearly at last. But then it is too late. The corn has ripened, but there is no friendly sickle at hand; the heart is bleeding, but no one cares to stoop and bind it up; the last faint spark of hope flickers out, and no cherishing hand tends and nurses the flame. We are alone, and we must abide alone till we can lift our eyes to heaven, and discover there the love which has been denied us on earth.

CHAPTER VIII.

THE MARCHESA.

KEITH'S rendezvous with the Marchesa at the Lido had really been unintentional. He had never supposed that, heedless of pearl-powder and complexion, she would expose her charms after a night's dissipation to the rays of the morning sun, and lose the opportunity of indulging in well-earned rest. He had not asked her to meet him, and it was a surprise, though naturally an agreeable one, when the Marchesa and her cousin, smiling under the shade of their broad-brimmed hats, greeted him cheerfully. No one could blame him if subsequently they had laughed and talked together. The Marchesa was essentially *bon enfant*, and an accomplished swimmer. She was as graceful and nimble as a fish, could

take mad headers from a little swaying boat,
dive and lie in most bewitching fashion, rocking on the waters, her full lips curved into a
smile as she gazed up at the blue heavens.
The display of her pretty gambols—though
perhaps Keith might not have approved of it
as an exhibition of his wife's prowess—was
naturally attractive to a man, and he returned
home with a light heart and a good appetite.
He felt perfectly innocent—his conscience reproached him with nothing; so that Dorothy's
jealous reproaches provoked him doubly, as
being most uncalled-for and disagreeable. It
was certainly far more difficult to please an
adored wife than a lively friend. Presents,
indeed, offered an easy solution of the matter;
but even presents might satiate, and in time lose
their soothing qualities. Thus Keith gloomily
reflected while he played at billiards, missing
the easiest canons, and twice blundering
over the particular stroke which had proved
generally infallible, till he eventually succeeded in losing two successive games.

'I can't play to-day,' he said impatiently,
throwing down his cue, which he pushed over
to Palis, who stood in his shirt-sleeves with a
cigar between his lips, looking fat and rosy
and the very impersonation of good-humour.

'Try your hand, old fellow, now; you will make more of it than I shall. I must take a stroll.'

'Take a stroll! why, it is raining cats and dogs! You must be more than commonly affected by the madness of the English to suggest such a thing!'

'It *is* raining,' said his friend, with a philosophic shrug of the shoulders, looking out of the window, and noting the large drops clinging to the pane and the wretched expression of a brown, bare-legged boy wedged up against the corner of a doorway, where he strove to find a scanty shelter from the storm. (A southern population always appear to look upon bad weather as a personal affront offered them by the Deity.) 'But I don't mind; it won't hurt me. I shall go and pay visits.'

Once in his gondola, no visit could appear so natural and pleasing as that to the Marchesa Bellaggio, on the plea of inquiring whether she was fatigued, if she had caught cold, and also with a view to trying over again the violin Romance of Svendsen, which on his last visit she had pronounced charming.

Keith soon found himself in her small red satin drawing-room, where she sat alone under a many - coloured venetian mirror, behind a very English-looking tea-table, on which stood a small silver tea-kettle emitting vapoury steam.

'Quelle chance!' said Keith; 'I never dreamt of finding you alone.'

'Because, I suppose, you did not wish it,' she answered languidly, holding out the tips of her fingers for him to kiss, in true Italian fashion.

'Of course I did. How can you suggest the contrary! I came purposely to know if you were fatigued with your exertions.'

'Swimming never tires me. It is so free and fairy-like an exercise—very different from the tramp in thick boots along a muddy road, which they tell me English ladies delight in.'

'*They* would swim too, if they could do it as well as yourself.'

Keith thought of Dorothy. What a pity she had no accomplishments! Then he took the cup of tea the Marchesa handed him, and at the same time gave one rash look into her sleepy, lustrous eyes—eyes that hid rapacity under languor, and selfish indolence under the air of tenderest appeal.

'Mrs. Chester is none the worse, I trust, for *her* exertions?'

As the Marchesa spoke she carefully poured cream into her cup, watching him furtively, but keenly, during the operation.

'She is a little tired, I fear;' and Keith sighed.

The Marchesa immediately suspected something beyond fatigue, and with joy scented an intrigue.

'Those fragile, ethereal - looking women can't stand much fatigue, I suppose; but then they have such advantages: their very fragility commends them to men's love and attention. Confess you could not care for a woman if she were not beautiful, gentle, dependent—appealing to that sense of power which is inherent in all men, but especially in *you*. Ah, I have watched you, studied you.' (Keith did not object to form an object of study to a pretty woman.) 'You have your vanity too, though it is well hidden away in that mysterious heart of yours. By the way, though, is not that a misnomer—*have* you a heart?'

'How can you ask, Marchesa? I am a victim to soft-heartedness.'

'You *make* victims, you mean. I wish I knew for a fact'—the Marchesa poised her head meditatively on one side—'I wish I knew. You are a riddle.'

' A riddle to which I am sure you possess the key,' said Keith gallantly, who believed compliments as necessary to a woman's happiness as cream to cats.

' I ? Mrs. Chester, you mean. She is the proper keeper of your heart ; and if I were in her place I should not let it lightly go from my care. Yet, do you know, there is something to-day in the air that impels me to confidence. Is it the *intimité* of the tea-table, do you think ? But to you, who know my sad fate—married at fifteen, un vrai bébé, to a man I could not love (how could I ? he is a nonentity, a peevish, sickly nonentity, a vegetarian. Can such have a loving heart and warm blood in his veins ? No, no!)—I must confess how much I have longed for a true marriage, a marriage of the heart—like yours! to belong by every tie that is most sacred and tender to one I could love passionately, who would be a guide, a help, a friend—for we women are *so* weak, and weakest when we love most—to share his companionship, his occupations, his thoughts. Ah, you will think me "tête montée." Yes, it *is* a dream, a dream of paradise—that one impossible ideal which each one raises, and each one in his turn is doomed to behold shattered at his feet. Well—somehow when I see you, and think of *your* happiness, these kind of dreams come to me. Is it not foolish? but then it is so innocent; and how seldom we women of the world can be innocent—like your sweet Dorothy!'

The Marchesa stopped; a tear glittered on her lashes. She shook back the deep-hanging lace of her sleeves and displayed a finely rounded arm. Her dress to-day was more than usually unconventional. She wore a loose robe of some soft Eastern silk, which seemed to have deliciously retained the sun's rays in its hues of golden-red, and which hung loosely about her, concealing the figure, and being cut open in a heart-shape at the neck, where it disappeared into floods of tawny lace. Keith had never before seen her in so gentle a mood, and her manner tinged with such graceful sweetness.

' Do not speak so, Marchesa!' he said ; 'you whom we all admire, all respect.'

' Respect is a cold word, Mr. Chester, and a true woman hates the cold ; she shrinks from it—for when *cold* touches the heart, it means *death.*'

The Marchesa was pale—too pale ; but her lips glowed red, and her eyes were full of light. The tea-table stood between her and Keith, with its air of homely comfort, while the rain pattered at the windows and the wind blew shrilly outside. People asserted that the Marchesa was artificial and designing. Keith thought her infinitely sympathetic. Why is it that experience so frequently teaches us to distrust our own inclinations?—though first impressions occasionally assert themselves with unpleasant pertinacity, and refuse to give way to reason or the warnings of friends.

Keith was a believer in the brotherhood of sympathy, and had often blamed his wife for her cautious method of making friends.

'I like to wait,' she would say, 'and get to know people.'

'And yet, you little fool, you loved me at first sight!'

'Ah, that was because I *was* a fool,' she said prettily. Then, with a sudden dash of remorse, 'No, you know I do not mean that—because love is love, and *you* are perfect.'

What had the recollection of this little matrimonial episode to do with the Marchesa and her large dark eyes, and her loveless marriage, and her yearnings, and Keith's presence at her tea-table? Nothing whatever, excepting that mental association plays us

strange tricks ; and that to-day both the
Marchesa and Keith dreamed dreams.   Dreams
not capable of interpretation like that of Pha-
raoh, nor yet possessed of any moral tendency,
nor yet innocent, as the airy imaginings of
rosy maidens in their morning slumbers ;
but dreams—impotent, idle, lying, wonderful
dreams !

Suddenly the red satin walls seemed to Keith
to part asunder, and to admit the cool vista
of a pale-green room with old-fashioned white
carvings, in which the fair head of a young
girl bent over her embroidery.   This mental
picture was painted in the purest and freshest
of colours ; and though Keith continued to
look into the Marchesa's dark eyes, he now
saw only clear blue orbs.   The picture indeli-
bly impressed on his memory from the first
day, restored the vividness of tender love and
of those ideas of purity and innocence that
had so charmed him at that period.   Was it
not Dorothy's guilelessness, the spotlessness
of her spirit and of her beauty, that had be-
witched him ?—and were not these qualities
as truly and completely hers as ever ?

Keith slowly withdrew his gaze from the
Marchesa's face ; but she, with the quick perception of a woman of the world, had already

noticed that his gaze was sightless, that his thoughts were not with her, that his dreams possessed no affinity to hers.

A constrained silence fell upon them. The red walls had closed again, and Keith knew but too well in whose presence he was.

When a woman has invited a man's confidence by proffering her own—when the offer has been doubtfully accepted, and instead of the warm welcome she anticipated, her little confessions have met with a cool reception—she is likely to feel aggrieved—angry, if you will. But the Marchesa's abandon did not comprise any absence of self-control; she had no intention of driving away her visitor by a silly display of temper. She wisely sheathed her weapons of war, and elected to wait for a better opportunity.

'Chance manquée, ce sera pour une autre fois,' was the mental comment with which she comforted her own impatience. Holding out her hand with the frank action of an understanding comrade, she said with a slight laugh :

'There! we have both of us been romancing like schoolgirls. Never mind—it is a pleasant and healthful amusement. I have wasted your time for you ; do you owe me a grudge?'

'Certainly not'—Keith rose at the clearly

expressed hint—'but I rather think it is late; so I will leave you.'

'Only to come again, I hope, for you have not played anything; and I was longing to hear the Romance. Well then, it must be for another day.'

'Of course, Marchesa. You know I will always play you anything you like;' Keith bowed himself out, completely the man of the world again. 'Time spent with you is always most agreeable.'

Nevertheless, Keith's feelings were somewhat of the order of his who said :

> 'He who fights and runs away,
> May live to fight another day.'

The rain had ceased, and he dismissed the gondola, proceeding to stroll slowly along the complicated network of narrow lanes and traghetti, which he knew so intimately.

'Poor Marchesa!' he thought; 'she *has* a heart, which makes it hard for her, though for me there is no danger ;' and, thus thinking, he repeated between his teeth those verses of Monckton Milnes, which somehow sounded appropriate to the situation:

> 'When along the light ripple the far serenade
> Has accosted the ear of each passionate maid,
> She may open the window that looks on the stream,
> She may smile on her pillow, and blend it in dream;

Half in words, half in music, it pierces the gloom,
I am coming—Stali—but you know not for whom.
                Stali—not for whom.

'Now the tones become clearer—you hear more and more,
How the water divided returns on the oar;
Does the prow of the gondola strike on the stair?
Do the voices and instruments pause and prepare?
Oh, they faint on the ear as the lamp on the view!
I am passing—Premè—but I stay not for you!
               Premè—not for you!

'Then return to your couch, you who stifle a tear;
Then awake not, fair sleeper—believe he is here.
For the young and the loving no sorrow endures;
If to-day be another's, to-morrow is yours.
May, the next time you listen, your fancy be there.
I am coming—Sciàr—and for you and to you!
              Sciàr—and to you!'

CHAPTER IX.

IN THE ROYAL GARDENS.

KEITH, from this day forward, gradually lapsed into the idle, lounging life which his long residence abroad rendered most congenial to him. The Marchesa was a good pianist, and it was astonishing how many hours she found it necessary to practise with Keith's violin. At other times he would saunter, talk, and pay compliments to the numerous pretty and fashionable women that clustered, clad in the most brilliant of summer garments, in the afternoon on the piazza, until he earned for himself the title, unanimously bestowed, of the most agreeable young man in Venice. The *dolce far niente* is a species of existence that grows upon its votaries. One hour spent in luxurious indolence makes it easier to dawdle away the next, until the slightest exertion becomes tedious.

Palis's bright sunny nature, and his gift of song, naturally caused him also to be drawn into the vortex of fashionable society, which is pretty much the same all over the world, being selfish in its pleasures, and insatiable in its demands for amusement. Palis pleased the company none the less by his show of indifference and careless philosophy; and his presence at all social gatherings soon proved indispensable.

Mrs. Chester, on the other hand, was not popular. That graceful mode of wasting time, while yet preserving the appearance of eternal business, remained a sealed mystery to her. The quiet village life, with its round of daily duties, had created in her a desire for something more satisfying than the chatter of coffee-parties. Besides, she had become thoroughly imbued with the true spirit of Venetian life—its dreamy soothing influences —its charm of varied colouring. Nothing pleased her better than to stroll through the busy market-place, and note the wondrous tints of fish and fruit, the gleams and glitter, the gold and silver sparkles, the ruddy fruit glowing in the baskets of the rosy

market women from Mestre, the wealth and
warmth of colour which, almost dazzling her
unaccustomed eyes, had once inspired a Titian
or a Paul Veronese. Occasionally, sated by the
gaudy show, she would stroll into some dusky
church, where the sacrament lay exposed on
the altar, and the priests knelt adoringly
before it, while the smell of incense filled the
heavy air.

Dorothy envied the faith which seemed
thus a part of the simple daily life, though she
could not share it. But sweetest of all to
her were the long expeditions in the swiftly
gliding gondola, which, now that Palis was
constantly engaged, she took alone with her
gondoliers, floating down narrow canals, where
the green waters lapped gently against marble
steps and moss-grown walls ; and through the
dim shadow of an arch gleamed the graceful
foliage of a vine or an acacia ; and bars of
golden sunshine suddenly struck the eye, or
snatches of melodious song fell upon the ear.
Long, lonely excursions did Dorothy make
thus, learning to love the solitude and the
silence.

One evening she wandered at the sunset
hour in the Giardine Reale. Keith and Palis
were dining out with a party of men, and

her time was her own. She had lingered
beyond the usual hour, feeling sad and listless.
Walking thus in the deserted gardens, now
forsaken by the fine ladies and dandies, with
their fans and parasols, where the air was
sweet with a thousand mingled scents, involuntarily she thought of the words of
Alfred de Musset, which Palis had once sung
to her:

> 'À Saint Blaise, à la Zuecca,
>   Vous étiez, vous étiez bien aise,
>   À Saint Blaise.
>   À Saint Blaise, à la Zuecca,
>   Nous étions bien là.

> 'Mais de vous en souvenir
>   Prendrez-vous, la peine?
>   Mais de vous en souvenir
>   Et d'y revenir.'

' " De vous en souvenir et d'y revenir," ' she
repeated slowly; ' already I, so young, have
memories—can I ever forget ?'

> 'À Saint Blaise, à la Zuecca,
>   Dans les prés fleuris cueillir la verveine:
>   À Saint Blaise, à la Zuecca,
>   Vivre et mourir là.'

How far off the old English life seemed
now; and yet how her very heart yearned for
it! If she could but persuade Keith to take
up his obvious duties as a landowner, to build
cottages, improve farms, and look after his
own tenants, they would then have mutual

interests, mutual tastes. But here, Dorothy sighed — companionship seemed impossible. Mrs. Maynard visiting dirty poor people and teaching little children, even against her will, appeared in the light of a saint compared to herself, wasting indefinitely the precious hours of existence.

At that instant the ardent glow of the descending sun attracted her attention. Sea and sky met in one sheet of flame, except where the line of shadowy buildings, their arrow-like cupolas and minarets pointing upward, formed a horizon; the vague violet mass, with the great light behind it, seeming to float in an incandescent lake. A wonderful stillness pervaded everything. The sea was confounded with the sky; the one appeared to reflect the other. All sense of existence felt unreal and vague; mystery encompassed her, life became spiritual, sublime. Then by slow degrees, like hope dying out, the brilliant colouring faded ; objects waxed misty and opaque, a grey haze filled the place of the gold and ruby gleams, and the air grew chill and cold.

Dorothy started from her dreams, unclasped the hands she had pressed closely together in her thrill of enthusiasm, and turned to seek her gondola. She found the place where she had left it, stepped lightly in without vouchsafing a glance at her attendant, so absorbed was she in her reverie, and, somewhat fatigued, leant back among her cushions.

The gondola shot swiftly out into the lagune, now a clear unbroken sheet of crystal, on which twinkling stars threw quivering images. The plashing of the water gently accompanied her thoughts ; she asked nothing better than to float thus onward in careless silence. But soon she noticed that their progress lay in the wrong direction; they were drifting out towards the pearl-grey sea. Venice and its twinkling lights lay behind instead of before them. In her pretty half-broken Italian she called out to the gondolier:

' You have not taken the right way ; I wish to return to the palace!'

At the sound of her voice a man crouching in the stern, whom she had not previously observed, stepped forward, and said in English :

' We are not going home just yet, for I have to speak to you.'

' What have you to say ?' asked Dorothy in sudden fear, for the night was coming, and she was never very bold, though the sense of

being accompanied by her own trusty servant
had hitherto given her courage in her lonely
expeditions.

'Do you not remember me?' said the
stranger, now approaching closer. 'I remember
you perfectly!'

'Why, I have never seen you!'

'You have indeed, on one occasion—
think!'

Dorothy shook her head. There was something in the calm insolent manner of this man,
his strange apparition, and her own un-
protectedness, which alarmed her exceedingly.

'Mrs. Parkinson introduced us,' he said;
'and I walked home with you one afternoon
at Dronington.'

'Then you are——'

'Elias F. Joynte, Mrs. Parkinson's *protégé.*'

'Why did you disappear so suddenly?
What are you doing here? What do you
want with me?'

Dorothy shrank visibly under the influence
of the sinister smile that curled the corners of
his mouth, where the scrubby black moustache
permitted it to be visible, and lurked in his
hard grey eye. Women, like dogs, instinctively and unerringly scent the presence of
danger.

'I shall tell you that presently ; but I want to talk about yourself first. You seem to enjoy Venice, but it is imprudent of you to go about alone—indeed, scarcely befitting a bride! Where is your husband to-night ?' he added roughly.

'He is dining out. I cannot listen to you any longer ; and, Mr. Joynte, I beg you to leave me.'

'Willingly, as soon as we reach dry land ; I have no wish for a swim. And meanwhile, as we are most agreeably alone together in the midst of this solitary lagune, I fear you will have to put up with my company; not to speak of the fact that, as I took the liberty of sending home your own gondola, this man is my paid servant. Observe, therefore, that you are in my power. We are a good way from Venice, and your screams would not be heard. I say this in order to warn you ; but I have not an idea of harming you. I only want to talk to you!'

Dorothy glanced helplessly round and resigned herself, seeing that opposition would be fruitless. The prow of the gondola was now set towards Venice, but the distance between them and the city remained considerable.

'Do you really not know the cause of my
disappearance that day ? You thought it was
generosity on my part, eh ?' he chuckled dis-
agreeably. 'Fear, then? idleness?—what?'

'I thought, simply, that you were unable
to substantiate your accusations,' she said
quietly, 'and that you had wisely retired.'

'Did you, now ? Well, it was nothing of
the sort!' Joynte's American twang increased
with his excitement. 'Mr. Chester *paid* me
to go!'

'It is false!' cried Dorothy, starting from
her seat, then sitting down again, with a sudden
remembrance of her position.

'Is it ? Ask him!'

He spoke with such a force of conviction
that for a moment she hesitated. There was
doubtless some strange misconception in all
this, which it was not her business to unravel;
but of one thing she was certain, Keith must
be innocent !

'I don't suppose you are quite so infatuated
now,' proceeded Joynte, 'as you were at that
time. It was not such a very satisfactory
marriage for you, after all. You seem to have
a good deal of spare time on your hands ; and
a young wife is naturally riled about that.
Such a pretty creature as you are, too!'

Dorothy winced. If the suspicion had never crossed her mind that it was not quite usual for young married women to spend their days in comparative solitude, at least she knew that to listen to a hint of such a thing from a man like Joynte was impossible.

'My affairs are my own!' she retorted with spirit. 'If you like to say anything about yourself—if I can help you'—she glanced doubtfully at his comfortable grey suit, and at the picturesque soft felt hat he wore—'I am ready to do so.'

'Thank you. I am not starving,' he said with a sneer. 'Still, you *can* help me. I wish you to be my ambassador with your husband. You have beauty, influence, I suppose—unless the Marchesa Bellaggio has robbed you of it all! He *must* listen to you! Tell him I want the remainder of the sum he promised me, and a little more besides. A fellow like me—a bit of an epicure—can't live on nothing. I am very fond of horses—I could breed them in my own country; but for that I must have capital.'

'If you have any claims on Mr. Chester,' said Dorothy firmly, beginning to recover from her alarm, and to resent the fact that her womanly compassion was being traded on, 'you had better write to him, or ask for an interview. I cannot take any messages; and this is in no way my business.'

'Do you refuse?' Joynte's voice trembled, but whether from passion or fear Dorothy had no means of judging, the whole of her energies concentrating themselves in a feverish desire to reach home quickly.

'Yes; I refuse.'

'Then, Mrs. Chester, I am sorry for you; but whatever evil consequences happen, must rest on your own head. Your husband is a _criminal!_ I could bring him to justice any day; but I should have held my tongue if you had obeyed my orders. I can tell you a strange story indeed; he——'

'I don't want to hear!' she put her hands to her ears to shut out the sound of his words. 'I don't want to know anything. You are a vile informer—the lowest thing in the world!'

'And you are a fool!' He seized her roughly by the arm; she thought he was going to harm her, and could scarcely repress a scream. 'But you will repent this, and one day come to me for mercy! I shall know everything that you do. I shall dog and follow you everywhere. You can't escape me! Do you still refuse?'

'Yes,' faltered Dorothy, feeling giddy with pain and excitement.

They were now in the midst of the city; lights were flashing, people talking and singing, boats passing. Joynte would dare nothing here, she believed. Very soon, indeed, though to her it seemed an eternity, the prow of the gondola grated against the marble steps of her palace, and Joynte cried harshly: 'Get out!'

She obeyed slowly, for her limbs were trembling under her. Once more she stood alone and safe at her own door, while the gondola floated off, and bore the men away into distance and obscurity. She waited a little before she summoned strength to ring the bell and lift the heavy brazen knocker. The servant, when he appeared, seemed surprised to see her thus alone.

'Is Mr. Chester come in?' she asked, striving to regain her usual composure and appear unconcerned.

Receiving an answer in the negative, she ordered some chocolate to be brought to her, lest her lack of appetite should excite suspicion, and hurried to her own room. She wanted to be alone; she wanted to think, to still the beating of her heart and the feverish excitement of her mind. First, however, she must endure the ordeal of Trimmer's attentions, suffer the assistance which she dared not refuse, listen to her questions as to what she required, during the slow process of disrobing. Then would come the refreshmenttray, and many tedious moments must elapse before Trimmer consented reluctantly to depart, and Dorothy remained free to hide her face in her hands and think.

Keith a criminal! What did it mean? The idea was ridiculous, impossible, foolish. Crime and gentility were decidedly incompatible—in fact, divided by an abyss—then her love returned with a strong, hearty gush. Keith, who was wise and clever, whose misfortune it was to be so perfect that universal admiration fell to his share and caused her jealousy—the very suggestion was treason to his good qualities. Never again would she be jealous, but, on the contrary, shield him from foul accusations, believe in him, try not to doubt him. It was envy that had originated these slanders, she was sure—envy of his beauty, his fortune, his happiness, of her love —and at this thought she smiled.

Now restored to her habitual calm, she rose and walked to the looking-glass, where she contemplated with disapproval her swollen features and her red eyes. She began to bathe them industriously, telling herself that dull looks could give no one happiness. Her well-meant efforts succeeded, for when Keith returned at a late hour, flushed and talkative, a serene and happy woman stood ready to welcome him. The sight was a contrast to the society he had just left, and his face beamed with agreeable surprise :

'Dorothy,' he said, 'how pretty you look! There is no one to compare with you. The fellows were deadly stupid to-night, and sang out of tune. After all, there is no place like home. Give me a kiss, dear, and tell me what you have been doing in my absence—sighing or fretting ?'

'Neither,' said Dorothy, as she threw herself on his breast, and nestled happily in his arms.

She did not breathe a word of Joynte's communication. It seemed to her as though suspicion were too vile a parasite to be permitted to exist near Keith, and that the mere mention of it would sully her pure lips. 'I trust him, and he trusts me,' she thought, and what do I care if all the world is against us?—no one can ever part us now.' The sense of irrevocable possession is occasionally the veriest two-sided sword, and cuts the deeper the closer it is pressed to a loving heart ; but to her at that instant it afforded inexpressible comfort.

CHAPTER X.

ON A TERRACE.

DOROTHY contrived to keep her fears and her sorrows to herself upon this occasion ; though afterwards in spare hours, of which she had many, and quiet moments, which her affluent position freely afforded her, they swooped down like a swarm of stinging insects upon her mind, and pricked and worried her. In one respect Joynte's accusations proved beneficial, for they caused her to attach herself with a greater pertinacity of affection to her husband, and to avoid all reproaches and jealous suspicions. Her sweet, well-balanced nature resumed its normal calm, and while she eagerly availed herself of every opportunity of enjoying her husband's society, she endeavoured to make herself as pleasant and necessary to him as possible.

Keith soon noticed this agreeable change, and readily profited by it without troubling to ask any questions. Joynte, indeed, appeared no more on the scene, though for many days Dorothy scarcely dared venture out of doors alone for fear of meeting him. People gradually began to desert Venice, and the English girl caught herself sighing for the shade of wide-spreading trees in her own native land. Not so Palis, whose mysterious mission to Venice lengthened indefinitely, like Penelope's task. He seemed to expand, to grow fatter and rosier and merrier with the heat, which relaxed and enervated everyone else. In his grey alpaca coat, loosely knotted tie, and wide white pantaloons, he sauntered about, provokingly cool and happy, blowing the cigarette-smoke in epicurean indolence from between his lips.

Keith, on his part, did not suffer from the heat, though it rather bored him. He had adopted as a relaxation the habit of passing a portion of the sultry day sometimes in playing the violin to the Marchesa's accompaniment, sometimes on the terrace of her palace, where the breezes blew in fresh from the sea, and the Marchesa herself lay, in a light thin garment, gently rocking in a hammock. No further confidences passed between them ; her matrimonial difficulties were only incidentally alluded to, as when she spoke of her husband's absence on their country estate, and remarked, ' that it was pleasant to be free to do as you liked in hot weather ;' or when, in answer to Keith's inquiry as to how much longer she intended to stay in Venice, she answered, ' I don't know ; I am very happy as I am. It is so dull in the country ;' adding, as she saw a question rising to his lips : ' There is only my husband there, you know. The house is too small for company, and the roads are bad.'

Keith understood all that was conveyed in these simple words, and made no further inquiry. He liked to see the Marchesa lying there, so handsome, so cool, and so good-humoured; he liked to talk and smile, or sit silent and listen to her pungent remarks on men and manners, and her original and independent views on the ' rational cultivation of pleasure,' as she termed it. ' I have the supremest contempt,' she asserted, ' for people who take their pleasure as children do their medicine, because it is given them. Now pleasure is a study. The first necessary is, that you should weed your society ; every-

body is not fit to enjoy. You must choose
your surroundings—your *scenery*, as they say
on the stage—and avoid fatigue, for satiety is
the grave of pleasure. In addition, there are
numberless other gifts that require to be cultivated: the senses of smell and taste, the
faculties of the eye, the ear, the nose—general
taste in fact, for the vulgar may stare and
grin and wonder, but they have no notion of
pleasure, which is a fine art not to be mentioned in the same breath with dissipation.'

Certainly, if the so-called fine art consisted in
making everyone else's comfort subservient to
hers, the Marchesa understood pleasure to
perfection; for while Keith quietly smiled at
her paradoxes, and she herself played with
her fan—lifting it gently, letting it drop
languidly, fluttering it coquettishly, waving it
mysteriously, closing it abruptly—she kept
Count Pinsuti ever on the trot carrying out
her behests. It was 'Count' here, 'Count'
there, 'Count' everywhere; the patient little
fellow trotting hither and thither, puffing,
perspiring, yet always obedient and devoted.
Naturally, with the impotent envy of an inferior
nature, he hated Keith, though he privately
cheered himself with the comfortable assurance
that the Marchesa's liking for the Englishman's

society was only transitory, the mere caprice of a pretty woman. To this end he determined to relax none of his efforts to please, and to continue to deserve her favour by making himself necessary and invaluable.

' How hot it is here,' she remarked one day to Keith, as she lay in her hammock among the orange and oleander bushes that grew in tubs on her terrace. ' I like it; the heat seems to infuse fresh life into me. No sun is too burning for my comfort—in fact, purgatory will have no terrors—but you suffer, I suppose. You look so hot, you poor creature, who come from a chilly country.'

' I don't mind it,' said Keith, though he gasped a little; ' but *he* ' (pointing to the Count's retreating figure) ' must find it hot and rather trying—you never let him sit still for a moment.'

' Exercise agrees with him,' said she airily ; ' he is like those dogs—retrievers, don't you call them?—who are never happy except when they are fetching and carrying. If he did not do that kind of thing for me, he would be doing it for some one else. People dilate on the wrongs of slavery—" je m'en moque bien "—some people are born slaves—and Count Pinsuti is one of them.'

'Do you think they like to be slaves?' said Keith pensively.

'Certainly; it is their nature. I don't much appreciate the species, but probably they have their interest and their use.'

'I suppose everything has its use?'

'Yes. Even *you* have your use. You have made my summer very agreeable to me.' She said this in a casual kind of fashion, quite as though it were not a bit of a complimentary speech; indeed, without pausing, she abruptly added, 'When do you leave Venice?'

'I really scarcely know.'

'Depends on your wife, I suppose,' she said, with a flirt of her fan.

'No, but——'

'On what then? you will scarcely lay the blame on *me*, I presume. Ah, Count'—this to the faithful servitor, who having returned, now stood patiently offering her a larger fan—'really I am very sorry; the breeze has risen; I don't think I feel hot now—in fact, a little chilly. Would you mind fetching me a shawl?' She accompanied these words with a bewitching smile, and the little man trotted off again immediately with a half-stifled sigh, previously wiping his face.

'There now, you see,' she said, triumphantly,

to Keith. 'I told you he *likes* it. But to
return, when *are* you going?'

'Are you anxious for my departure?'

'I think you can guess whether I am; but
sometimes an unpleasant certainty is preferable
to uncertainty.'

'I will stay till you bid me go.'

'And your wife?'

'Married people are one. What pleases
me, pleases her.'

'Verily, a model couple.'

The Marchesa lifted her eyebrows, turned,
and resting herself on her elbow, gave him a
queer unbelieving look. 'Mrs. Chester does
not like me; she scarcely ever pays me a visit
now.'

'An omission, I am sure,' he said hastily.
'I will tell her—it is pure forgetfulness.'

'Don't trouble yourself. Your wife is no
fool, and you make a mistake in treating her
as if she were; she is a clever woman.'

'Yes?'

'Don't look incredulous: she is, I tell you,
a clever woman; and she loves you, consequently has sharp eyes. I should not like
Mrs. Chester for a rival. She is just one of
those women who say nothing, keep very
quiet and mum, and suddenly swoop down

upon you, when you least expect it, with some overwhelming piece of diplomacy.'

'Dorothy is no diplomat. She is simplicity itself.'

'Who said she wasn't? Simplicity is the most consummate art, and the keenest weapon of women and diplomats. Believe me, you don't half understand your wife; but you are not singular—not every husband does understand his wife.'

Keith resented this summary disapproval, feeling it to be a subtle commentary on his intelligence, and naturally preferring to believe himself above the ordinary run of fools. At the same time he was anxious to propitiate the Marchesa, yet not desirous of discussing his wife's faults or perfections. The Marchesa noticed his annoyance, and inwardly rejoiced. The little Count at that instant reappearing, she signed to him to approach and pour out some sirop and iced water that stood on the tray beside her. She took the glass from his hand, and as she did so, slowly lifting it and looking into his face the while—

'Your health, Count; drink mine now, for you must be thirsty, and our pensive Englishman also. Shall I drink to *your* health, Mr. Chester, and that of your fair wife?'

' As you please, Marchesa; good wishes are
never to be despised. But your sirop is too
sweet for me. May I have cognac and seltzer-
water instead?'

Keith returned home somewhat moodily
inclined, to find Dorothy more than usually
merry. At dinner she bantered him gaily,
and even asked kindly after the Marchesa.
Keith sipped his hock, thought her more than
commonly pretty, and wondered in his own
mind if she were a diplomat. The cool white
garments she habitually wore brought into
relief her golden hair and fair complexion.
Her face was bent over her plate, and her eyes
fixed on the rosy peach she was preparing for
his delectation.

' There, dear, it looks very juicy;' she said,
handing it him nicely peeled, with a spoonful
of sugar. ' And now, who do you think I
have heard to-day is coming here?'

' Who?' he asked, with his mouth full, drawing her towards him and making her perch on
the arm of his chair. ' Your mother and sister?'

Dorothy laughed.

' I can't imagine *their* starting off on so
long a journey. No, it is the dearest and best
of women—I mean, of course, except mamma
and Margaret, who are dearer and better still.'

' Who is it, then?'

'Keith, you will delight in her, I know—have some more sugar, dear? You will like her so much. I only hope I shan't be jealous of Lady Darlington.'

'Oh! is it Lady Darlington?'

'Yes—don't look grave—she and Lord Darlington will be here immediately, and she has asked me to order their rooms at the hotel.'

'Stuck-up English swells, I suppose they are; and that is what you think charming!'

'They are not stuck-up; she is a little dear, and I have always heard he is a good fellow.'

'Hunts, doesn't he?'

'Yes, keeps hounds, and knows such a quantity about everything in the country; and they have besides such charming children. Keith, I wonder whether you like children; I don't think I ever asked you.'

She laid her face against her husband's cheek, so that he was forced to put down his wine-glass to kiss her.

'Yes—Lady Darlington is a perfect woman,' she said presently; 'I like her exceedingly.'

'Some one else is perfect, too,' he said effusively; though he wondered a little bit whether all this talk of Dorothy's were not diplomacy, and if she were holding up the Darlingtons to him as an example to be copied

—a kind of grown-up edition of the good boys and girls in tracts, who never did anything wrong, and lived happy ever after.

Notwithstanding the doubts sown in his mind by the Marchesa's clever innuendoes, he still believed in Dorothy's simplicity, still credited her with no after-thoughts.

'What brings the Darlingtons here at this season?' he asked; 'the gaieties of London are scarcely over.'

'Oh, they do not care for gaieties. The hounds are the most troublesome things in their establishment—everything has to be regulated by them; and it seems July is a month when nothing particular is required—there is no regular hunting nor cub-hunting—only an occasional show of hounds, and Lord Darlington has for once consented to miss them.'

'How knowingly you talk!'

'Because, you see, I have heard of all this from Lady Darlington. I don't know much of him except that he is a bold rider, a great judge of hounds, and that Lady Darlington adores him——'

'And so you think I shall adore him too—eh, Dorothy?'

'Not necessarily. But men—Englishmen—always seem to have a kind of freemasonry amongst themselves by which they at once find mutually interesting topics of conversation; and I am sure you cannot have much in common with these Italian men.'

Keith stroked his moustache and smiled.

'Nor, perhaps, shall I have much in common with Lord Darlington. I rather dislike men who can talk of nothing but horses and hounds.'

'Keith dear, you will try to like him, for my sake, won't you?' she said earnestly, unable to banish the secret hope from her mind that somehow Lord Darlington's advent might lead to a return to England, that again to Keith's becoming a practical landlord and a resident in the country, a result culminating in the realization of her dream—to have a wider, happier sphere of life. These vague enthusiastic visions floated now unceasingly before the mind of the fair English girl, leaving her no rest as she sat in her palace at Venice, surrounded by treasures of art, satiated already with the gorgeous colouring of nature, the sunsets and moonlight effects. Her head, full of sundry similar cogitations, was just now pillowed on the shoulder of the handsome man whom she called husband, but of whose inner soul-experiences and former mode of life she remained profoundly ignorant.

CHAPTER XI.

IN A GARRET.

ELIAS F. JOYNTE was an American by birth, but he was also a member of that vast human family whose whole existence is one gigantic grievance, whose heart and thoughts and faculties gradually rot themselves away in aching envy and disappointment. He was young, he was ambitious, and he was discontented. From the day when, as a mere lad, he had been told by some idle busybody that his cousin Ida Phaer, heiress to the family wealth, seemed a likely match for him, until the day of her death as Keith's betrothed, when the discovery was made that she had left the latter all her fortune, Joynte had felt that his life was a mistake—felt it and chafed under the sensation until he almost went mad.

Quite mad, the authorities averred, when, under Keith's advice, they locked him up in a mad-house. Latterly he had attained his liberty, but never his freedom of mind; he still lived only under a kind of protest, he was still haunted by a terrible fear of incarceration in those dreadful prison-walls, still driven to lead a kind of skulking, frightened existence. Moreover, since his interview with Dorothy he kept pretty closely hidden, stealing out only at night, or else to seek his food in one of the low trattoria of the neighbourhood.

He had found himself mistaken in his estimate of Dorothy's character, having fancied she would possess a timid nature, nervous excitability, and a weak vacillating disposition in accord with her blonde and fragile appearance. He had hoped she would succumb to his threats at once—agree to his terms, and offer him a large sum of money for silence. Instead, making all due allowance for a first thrill of natural feminine fear, he discovered her to be calm, self-possessed, and full of logical common-sense. True, he had still the option of holding over her head the threat of unknown terrors, which by their very vagueness have power to quell the lustiest courage;

yet how was it possible to be sure that she might not impart her fears and indignation to her husband? who in that case would promptly proceed to immure Joynte again as a maniac, perhaps even, if he had threatened her, as a dangerous one.

It was for this reason that, having played his trump-card, and made the appeal to Mrs. Chester, he now remained in the seclusion of private life in a garret. The two hundred pounds given by Keith, together with the small sums he had extracted from Mrs. Parkinson's good-nature, had by this time almost entirely melted away : forty pounds alone having been frittered in a week's insensate dissipation among boon companions on his way through Paris.

Elias was not a drunkard by nature, nor a riotous liver, but he had a gift for dribbling away money : he dribbled it chiefly in company, and probably enjoyed it less than the associates who laughed at him for his pains ; but there was a kind of almost pathetic generosity about the man, inducing him to stand treat on all occasions, when he had anything in his pockets. Fortunately, Venice was a place in which one could live economically—where butcher's meat was an unneces-

sary luxury, and there was nothing to pay
for sunshine.

In order to arrive at Joynte's abode, it
became imperative to plunge into a labyrinth
of narrow alleys, each bearing the closest family
resemblance, until you reached a tall flesh-
coloured house, with dilapidated green shutters,
off which the paint peeled in flakes, and
which, whenever there was any wind, flapped
uneasily on a set of rusty hinges. The lower
part of the house consisted of a small general
shop, the wares of which were chiefly displayed outside, the inside being stifled in dirt
and darkness, and encumbered by strings of
tallow-candles, baskets of gourds, bundles of
dried seeds, mouldy-looking cheese, etc. ; and
lighted dimly, only in the far background, by
a wick burning in a saucer of oil, before a
hideous little plaster Virgin, decked out in
tinsel and pink paper.

The presiding genius of the shop, a fat
Jewess, with gold necklace and earrings,
passed a great portion of her time seated in
the doorway bargaining with customers, but
apparently seldom able to conclude a satisfactory transaction, which reduced her means
of livelihood to an interesting mystery.
Possibly her lodgers contributed no incon-

siderable item to the domestic revenue ; for up a dark, rickety stair, smelling strongly of grease and garlic, you eventually attained to a couple of garrets, one of which was, at the present moment, occupied by Joynte. Here, under the tiles, sweltering in the baking July sun, he sat smoking in a dirty shirt, leaning his arms upon the window-sill, whence hung a few gaudy rags, and a crimson carnation drooping its heavy scented head far below the pot in which it grew, as though thoroughly ashamed of its humble position, and yet unable to conceal aught of its beauty and its fragrance.

Here Joynte sat and ruminated the livelong day, looking down with sullen eyes upon the busy street-life below ; upon the fruit-sellers, and the gondoliers lounging, spitting, and lolling against the doors of the wine-shop at the corner ; at the Jews, with their shabby clothes, their greasy looks, and aquiline noses, cringing rapidly by ; and the sailors, with their bronzed faces and long earrings, laughing with pretty girls in brilliant-coloured handkerchiefs and shawls. He sat brewing bitter hatred and resentment within him, and longing to find some means of wreaking his revenge.

CHAPTER XII.

LADY DARLINGTON.

LORD and Lady Darlington had indeed arrived in Venice. Lady Darlington brought with her a maid, a fat pug, and a collection of photographs of her darling children, in every variety of size and attitude, little Letty's first tooth mounted in gold and hanging to her watch-chain, and a bit of Hetty's golden hair in a locket round her neck. Her pocket and travelling-bag contained a bundle of letters received at different stages of the journey from nurses and governesses, with the latest reports of the state of health and spirits of the children, and abounding in such details as the variations of the weather, and the increase or decrease of the infant's appetite.

Lord Darlington brought with him a valet

and a courier, his kennel-book, stud-book, and
Bailey's Magazine, which proved an engross-
ing study at all times, both convenient and inconvenient—in railway trains, during tedious
halts at wayside stations—in the suite of dull
and solemn hotel apartments, where a large
gold clock and a pair of candelabras formed
the chief ornament and decoration, yet for
which ninety francs a day were charged, in
honour of the fact that the English family
were a milord and a milady of the very
highest rank (the courier took care to impress
this on everyone he met), and understood
little else but English, which, while a trifle
inconvenient in foreign travel, yet proved their
high distinction, and that they were the kind
of people who counted accomplishments as a
secondary consideration.

On this the evening of their first arrival in
Venice, it being then past the usual English
dinner-hour, to which, whenever possible, they
religiously conformed, they sat in the vast
palatial apartment prepared for them ; my
lady busy arranging the children's photographs, and my lord on the sofa, reading the
last accounts received of hounds and horses
from the stud-groom.

' All well at home,' said he presently, laying

down his letters and making room for my lady beside him on the sofa. 'Swivel says the roan is sound again, and Warrior is going like smoke. Duchess's puppies will be magnificent, marked just like their father, and already as game as possible; there isn't a scrap of distemper in the kennel. He is having Spilikins broken in for you; so, thank God, that's all good news.'

'He doesn't say anything about the children, does he?' said her ladyship, with a touch of anxiety in her tone.

'Not a word. But his letter was written before the telegram you received this morning, so it is all right.'

'Of course,' she said pensively, 'telegrams *are* quicker than letters, but they are not so satisfactory. Dear little Letty had a slight cold when nurse wrote, and I particularly wanted to know if she had tried the linseed-tea.'

'The hay is all safely in, and the crops look beautiful, Swivel says. If we have an early harvest we shall begin cub-hunting comfortably; but I wish to goodness I could have been there to superintend the laying out of the new thorn covert. They are sure to make a precious muddle of it without me.'

'It was very good of you, dear, to take me for this trip,' said his wife, affectionately slipping her hand through his arm ; ' because I know what a quantity of things there are for you to do at home.'

'Never mind, Nina, for once, though it is a nuisance about the thorn covert. Foreign countries altogether are a mistake, I think. The champagne was abominably sweet in Paris; and I never saw such a way as they farm abroad—the land divided into those absurd little patches, sometimes only an old woman to dig them ; the barbarous lingo they talk, too. However, I suppose it is all right ; and one must travel occasionally.'

'You are the dearest and best of fellows in the world,' said Lady Darlington effusively ; 'I really wanted very much to see Dorothy settled in her palace. It sounds so funny—a palace for ordinary mortals ! But I shall never ask you to come abroad again—at least, not until little Letty is older, and we can take *her*. We must show her the world, you know, Buffie.' (This was her husband's pet name, given him during his brief period of feather-bed soldiering, and used by his comrades as a diminutive for his title of Lord Burfleet.)

'I suppose we must,' he said regretfully ;

'but anyhow, we will choose a time when there are no confounded thorn coverts to be made.'

Lord Darlington might have been born in those prehistoric times when we are told 'there were giants in the land.' He was of such abnormal stature, so big and so bluff; and yet so genial and gentle withal, that women and animals felt no fear of him, and indeed generally loved him. Though his limbs were gigantic and his strength exceptional, his face was as innocent as a child's. Keen grey eyes looked out at you from beneath the broad honest brow, and the complexion, rosy and clear from early hours and constant exposure to fresh air and cold water, glowed with the freshness of early youth. On this account perhaps it was that little children unblushingly twined themselves round his legs whenever they found the opportunity, and dogs and cats purred and wagged their tails or leapt upon him, with the innocence and sense of protection peculiar to the young and undeveloped of their species.

It was a sight to see when he appeared in the hunting-field, smiling and serene, in his neat scarlet coat, and riding one of his hand-

some horses, took his place in the midst of
the joyous hounds, with their banner-like
waving tails. How the farmers touched their
hats, the gentry came quickly up and wished
him good-morning, the ladies bowed from
pony-carriages, and even the small boys holding open gates pulled with a will at their
forelocks in token of respect, with perhaps a
lurking expectation of halfpennies!

He had a word and a smile for all, so that
while his equals respected, his inferiors adored
him. He was so profoundly simple and so
profoundly just—two qualities that are often
found together ; so conscious of his own
duties and privileges, so unconscious of his
dignity ; so tolerant of his own rights, and yet
so interested in all the sorrows of his poorer
neighbours ; such a *man*, and, above all, such
a gentleman, as to make the veriest Socialist
pause and think better of it in his bitter abuse
of the aristocracy.

Little Lady Darlington, with difficulty
hoisting herself as high as his arm, looked
up proudly in his face and worshipped him.
These two simple people, surrounded by their
children, their dogs, and their horses, and
absorbed in uneventful country pursuits, were
perhaps the most unintellectual and happiest

couple in existence—a fact that might seem
subversive of the prevailing doctrine that
knowledge is power—they had so much influence in their way, and so little book-
learning.

Lord Darlington was usually habited in a
suit of grey homespun, breeches and gaiters
complete, the product of his own mill; but
on the occasion of his visit to Italy he so far
deferred to public opinion as to wear trousers
instead of breeches, still retaining, however,
the grey material. It would have been therefore impossible, as he stalked through the
streets of foreign cities, attired in this easy
and unconventional costume, to mistake him
for anyone but a born Englishman; and indeed he would violently have resented being
treated like a foreigner, for whom and his
ways he cultivated the supremest contempt,
saying in his loud, hearty tones, to which his
little wife cried vainly, 'Hush!':

'An Englishman is worth a dozen foreigners
any day, and will fight them all round—he
will, indeed, by Gad!'

This innocent bravado not appearing to
injure anyone—the foreigners in question being
indifferent to insults they could not understand, and continuing, like the silly creatures

they were, to tear off their hats, make room for madame, and grimace according to their ridiculous usage—gradually the young lord's martial ardour expired, and he began to look with a more favourable eye upon the renowned objects the courier pointed out as worthy of notice, being even finally persuaded into admiring the strange and stately aspect of the Queen of the Adriatic.

'Poor benighted creatures!' he was heard to say; 'fancy their taking all this trouble to build a town in the middle of the sea, where . there is not even a pack of hounds within reasonable distance!'

On the morning after their arrival, when the gondola sent by Mr. Chester appeared to convey them to their friend's palace, where they were expected to breakfast, Lord Darlington sarcastically eyed the conveyance and exclaimed :

'The hansom of Venice! Slow and inconvenient, very; damp, too, but cheap; a saving in horseflesh and extra helpers, very likely!'

'I think it is lovely,' said his wife ; 'and does not shake a bit. Oh, Buffie, you must give me one for our lake at home; it would be so nice!'

'And import one of these fellows, too, I suppose?' he said, surveying the gondoliers. 'No, I thank you; I much prefer an English coachman who thoroughly understands his business.'

During the time occupied in traversing the space between the hotel and the palace, Lord Darlington gave vent to various other derogatory remarks about the economy of a gondola; such as, 'that they were dingy-looking articles at best, and that the canals did not seem particularly odorous, and that no man could keep his figure if he were always to be punted about in this ridiculous fashion. How, indeed, did the people ever get exercise? No wonder the women grew fat and the men flabby!' at which Lady Darlington laughed, and then vowed she could see a great deal of poetry in it, though perhaps in time it might become a trifle monotonous; besides which, she was not quite sure whether Venice would be healthy in the long-run, certainly not for children.

And thus, in the most amiable of tempers, the pair arrived, were received in the vast cool hall by le Goui himself, more impressive and condescending than usual; slipped a little on the polished parquet of the long gallery, and finally reached Mrs. Chester's boudoir.

Then the two ladies rushed into one another's arms with exclamations of:

'How are you, dear? How nice you look! Not a bit changed.' 'So kind of you to come!' 'A nice cool dress! Paris, is it?' 'And the children all well, I hope?' while the gentlemen, in their more sober fashion, contented themselves with shaking hands.

Then all four, the ladies having finished their embraces, looked at one another in silence, as though much surprised and a little embarrassed at the meeting—as is the habit of English people. Finally Lord Darlington, in the tone of one imparting valuable information, said:

'Uncommonly fine weather for the harvest!'

'Very hot,' echoed his dutiful wife, with a pant.

'The usual weather here,' said Keith airily, while Dorothy drew her friend into a cool corner of the apartment.

Presently Palis appeared, and then further presentations took place, which were cut short by a summons to the breakfast-table.

'You call this breakfast?' said Lord Darlington; 'I call it dinner, all except the soup. What stomachs foreigners must have!'

'We eat less often here than in England,'

Keith said, with a smile, as he noticed that his guest's appetite was excellent; 'and the food is lighter.'

'Your cook has not yet quite attained to the true Provençal seasoning, however,' said Palis deliberately.

Lady Darlington looked up surprised; and Palis, imagining she was asking for salt, hastened to offer it, and, in so doing, upset the contents of the salt-cellar.

'Never mind!' he cried, gallantly pouring some claret over the snowy mound on the table-cloth. 'I will soon make it all right. There, I forgot; what have I done? I knew claret and salt were connected somehow.'

The decorous le Goui here interposed and speedily restored order, while Palis let off a few conversational fireworks in the shape of paradoxes in order to divert the attention of the company.

'Is there any society here?' asked Lady Darlington, when she found a favourable opportunity. 'I should so like to see some fine Venetian ladies.'

Her ladyship's mind was evidently a little hazy: she had visions of Titianesque beauties, with ruddy waving hair, wearing velvet gowns and stomachers of precious stones.

'There are several here—beauties—would you prefer a Marchesa or a Contessa?' said Palis; while Lady Darlington, unacquainted with the foreign titles, wondered what he meant. 'I should recommend the only Marchesa in Venice now for your inspection. Chester can tell you all about her; he plays the violin with her every day.'

Lady Darlington, looking up questioningly, intercepted a flash of appealing reproach sent across the table by Dorothy, and the little lady immediately decided upon her after-breakfast chat. She had not long to wait, for Mrs. Chester almost immediately suggested that they should take coffee in her boudoir, and while the gentlemen smoked their cigarettes Lady Darlington and herself should inspect the palace. Dorothy had not been long in her friend's presence before she felt the old sense of peace and comfort steal over her, and the old faith and trust return. Lady Darlington did her duty bravely: she admired marqueterie and buhl cabinets, and old Venetian mirrors, and silver caskets, and valuable embroideries, looked at the view from Dorothy's bedroom window, and examined the fine old quilt sewn with lilies, not caring a fig about any of these things, but only longing for the moment to arrive when she might draw forth Dorothy's confidence, and hear, as she mentally expressed it, ' all about everything.'

' How happy you must be, dear,' she said, when at last they came to an anchorage on the low sofa in the boudoir, beside which stood the table with the steaming coffee in quaint *capo-di-monte* cups, and the liqueurs in the thinnest of Murano glasses.

' How delightful — how interesting Mr. Chester is, and how beautiful your palace—you have everything you wish for. We shall never get you home again, I suppose?'

' I should be very happy to come home,' said Dorothy, with a sigh. ' Have you seen mother and Margaret lately? It seems to me such an age since I spoke to them. One seems to make such an enormous stride of time in a moment after one is married.'

' Have you many friends here?' said Lady Darlington abruptly.

' None, that I care for.'

' Not even the Marchesa, of whom they were speaking?'

' Certainly not.'

' But she is an old friend of your husband's?'

' I believe so.'

Dorothy turned away her head, but her

persistent little friend, seizing her by the chin, twisted it round so as to obtain a good view of her eyes.

'Dorothy, what is the matter?'

'Nothing, Lady Darlington, I assure you.'

'There is, though. Why don't you make a friend of this woman?'

'I don't know.'

'You do. Tell me, dear.'

'Because ——'

'Well, why?'

'Because I hate her! There! the murder is out; now please forget all I have said, for—oh! here are the gentlemen; for heaven's sake don't betray me, for I think,' and her voice sunk to a whisper, 'I think Keith rather likes her.'

CHAPTER XIII.

WHAT LADY DARLINGTON THOUGHT.

ITTLE Lady Darlington lapsed into unusual silence after receiving this confidence, while inwardly deciding that if *she* could help it, matters should not remain *in statu quo*. Alone with her husband, on the return journey, skimming the waters in ghostly fashion—the silent moving gondola plunging one moment into deep mysterious shadow under arches that looked as if they might serve the purpose of an entrance into hell; at other times emerging into silvery moonlight, almost as bright as daylight, only far colder and chillier, and less sympathetic—she slipped her tiny chubby hand into her husband's big one and sighed.

'Tired, dear?' he said, puffing at his big cigar. 'Sight-seeing is very fatiguing, and to my mind one church is exactly the same as another.'

' Yes,' said Lady Darlington absently, her mind wandering far from sights and wonders, for which, indeed, she had but a very partial admiration, laboriously cultivated, though regarding it as a solemn duty to ' read up ' Murray conscientiously, and to listen to all the explanations offered by garrulous and silver-coin-loving cicerones.

' Buffie,' she hazarded again, easing her anxiety by another sigh.

' Yes,' he said. ' What is it?'

' I want to speak to you.'

' Speak away; I am listening.'

' Not here ; when we reach the hotel,' with a shy glance in the direction of the gondoliers.

' They can't understand a word of English,' said her lord contemptuously.

' I don't know. They may, perhaps. Besides, these canals at night are so creepy. What was that gave a splash—a rat ?—or was it some one trying to drown himself? It is dreadfully lonely and mysterious here.'

' Nonsense, little woman ! I can only see a set of mouldy old houses, with moss growing up their sides, though I am aware of a strong smell of dirty water.'

Her ladyship here relapsed into a silence which she preserved unbroken until they reached the hotel and were once more safely installed in the palatial apartment with its painted frescoes of life-size gods and goddesses, its stiff velvet-covered furniture, and its large gold clock occupying the chimney-piece, on which the photos of the children were distributed with a lavish hand.

Lord Darlington mixed himself a tumbler of whisky and soda-water, lighted another large cigar, then, settling his huge limbs in one of the armchairs, looked inquiringly at his wife.

She again said 'Buffie,' and stopped.

'Well?' he said encouragingly.

'Buffie, I am unhappy about Dorothy.'

'Already? It seems rather unnecessarily early, especially as you are already troubled about Letty's cold. I think Chester capital company. You had not led me to expect half so good a fellow; fond of hunting—nice light-weight too. Told me all about the Roman hunting. Says he shall buy some horses, and ask my opinion about them first, when he returns to England. His wine and cigars, too, are excellent. Altogether, I should say it was a very well managed establishment.'

'Do you really think so? Well, I always maintain I had rather have your opinion about people than that of any one. else I know. You are such an accurate judge.'

'Habit, my dear; when a man is always judging hounds and horses, it makes him sharp and observant.'

'But really, Buffie,' her ladyship spoke diffidently, for Lord Darlington's opinion always inspired her with the deepest respect, 'on this occasion I don't think you have given enough attention to the subject. Think over it a little. The facts are——'

'I know. Pretty little girl, countrified, a trifle too pale and thin for my taste.'

Here Lady Darlington smiled consciously, for her own *embonpoint* caused her many anxious moments, the longest walks and rides seeming to make not the slightest impression upon it.

'He married for love, of course, for the girl had not a shilling ; she had never seen another man, and there was a bit of bravado about it, and spite of her mother and relations. Keith Chester is a man of the world—sensible fellow; she is a little schoolgirl ; finds marriage not quite the bit of silly sentimentality she expected; naturally confides this to a friend of her youth. A dozen children will soon settle that little difficulty, my dear.'

Lord Darlington stopped, out of breath, after this lengthy speech.

'It isn't exactly that,' said Lady Darlington. 'I am afraid Mr. Chester is not all he should be; that Marchesa we heard about——'

'Is *that* the way the wind blows?' said her husband, emitting a prolonged whistle. 'If so, Chester is a fool; it is early days for him to tire of his love-match. My dear, I can't believe it. Women are so impressionable, you know. So she told you this, did she?'

Lord Darlington took the cigar from his mouth, and remained absorbed in thought.

'She told me a little; but we were soon interrupted. I think—I am sure she is miserable. *I* should be, I know, if you looked too much at another woman.' Little Lady Darlington shuddered at the mere idea.

'Not likely, is it, Nina?' and he pinched her cheek affectionately.

'But what shall I do, Buffie?' pursued the affectionate creature, stroking the sleeve of his grey tweed suit.

'Nothing, do nothing,' he said emphatically. 'Least said soonest mended, and don't, above

all, encourage confidences. For my part, I
could see nothing unhappy about her. She
laughed and talked as merrily as a colt neighs
all breakfast-time.'

'Yes, with that absurd man Palis. I
laughed too. What an oddity he is! But
one may laugh and yet be miserable. I have
often laughed and cried in the same breath;
for instance, when Letty tumbled off her
pony, and I cried because I thought she was
hurt, and then I laughed when I found she was
not hurt, and looked such a little queer object
covered with mud; oh yes, I know how it
feels. Buffie, dear, I think *you* might do a
great deal for poor Dorothy.'

'Go on—what shall I do?'

'Talk to Mr. Chester; you know how
popular you always are with men; be nice
and friendly to him, persuade him to go back
to England and live on his property; it is so
much more natural, you know. They could
travel with us—that would be delightful—and
once in England, Dorothy would be among
her own people, and the Marchesa out of sight
and out of mind. I know what it is to be at
home; but a palace isn't a home—there's no
one cares for you, there's no farm, no garden,
no poultry-yard, no poor people——'

'You have the sentiments of a true Briton —there's no place like home, eh? Well, I'll see what I can do; will that satisfy you?'

'Oh yes,' and she seized him round the neck and gave him a good hug. She did not believe that any affair Lord Darlington felt inclined to interfere in could long remain a tangle, for she knew what excellent common-sense he possessed, and how quickly he disposed of any quarrels that occurred in the hunting - field, actually accomplishing the herculean task of pleasing every one and yet of upholding the right. So she quickly reassured herself about Dorothy, and went to sleep that night a happy and contented little woman.

The following morning she was up betimes, staring out of the French window, which stood open, at the strange and varied sights that met her eye: fisher-boats, with orange sails, carrying crabs, shell-fish, and sea-fruit of all kinds, guarded by tawny-limbed ear-ringed fishermen; gondolas stationary, with their attendants brushing, dusting and tidying, or gondolas moving, filled with ladies, chiefly English, wearing blue veils and carrying 'Murrays;' distant cupolas glittering in the sun, market-women with baskets of peaches, peasants—a motley array; and while she looked on with interest, listening to the hoarse, unintelligible cries and guttural squabbles, mentally wishing Lord Darlington would make haste and dress, so that they could start for the Chesters' palace and put their little diplomatic action in train at once. At last his lordship appeared, ruddier and fresher than ever, straight out of his cold bath, like a giant refreshed.

'I am so glad you have come at last. I have been waiting for you so long; do make haste, dear, and have your breakfast, that we may go off at once to the Chesters'.'

But his lordship was in no hurry. He ate his breakfast leisurely—meat and eggs and ham, just as if he were in England—washed down with claret-and-water, and then he smoked his cigar and read his letters, and found there were two or three he must answer, which he accordingly did in a rough and clumsy writing, getting very hot, and giving vent to a great many sighs over it, besides inking his fingers and his pocket-handkerchief. All this while his wife stood by, inwardly chafing, and volunteering her assistance, which was as persistently refused.

'Do let me write for you, dear,' she pleaded, 'I can do it in half the time.'

'Not a bit of it. Swivel wouldn't understand it at all if he didn't see my fist, and there are a whole lot of orders about the mares and the foals, which I must explain myself carefully.'

The letters over, his lordship dallied still to read the latest accounts of racing, and the prospects of the harvest, in the morning paper, having concluded which, he was at last persuaded to fetch his hat and to follow her ladyship, who, by this time, sat like a statue of patience in her gondola, shading her face from the burning sun with a white cotton parasol. It was the hottest part of the afternoon, for Lord Darlington had not hurried himself with his preparations, and at this hour Keith was wont to take the air and indulge in musical and artistic talk on the Marchesa's terrace. Palis glibly imparted to them this information, when the couple landed at the steps of the Chesters' palace and confronted him, cool, cheerful and unconcerned as usual.

'I am going there myself presently,' he added; 'if you like to be introduced I'll take you. She's a very handsome woman, the Marchesa, and capital company—quite a favourable specimen of Italian aristocracy. Will you come?'

Lady Darlington threw an anxious, inquiring glance at her husband. What if he too were to be inveigled in the enchantress's toils? His lordship hesitated a moment.

'Well, I've no objection; I haven't a thing on earth to do here. My wife can stay with Mrs. Chester meanwhile, and we shall all be back to dinner.'

'Which I have taken the precaution to order,' said Palis.

'Well, I suppose it must be so,' said Lady Darlington resignedly, as much as to say, 'I can't help myself, but I feel this is a temptation of the devil's, and ought to be resisted, if you only understood.'

The two men then bowed and departed, leaving the little lady alone on the doorstep, with le Goui regarding her admiringly. She heaved another sigh—the third the poor soul had emitted in the last twenty-four hours— then turned and followed the well-bred servant into Dorothy's presence.

'You have come alone,' said the latter warmly, rising from a low chair and looking like some gentle violet near a gorgeous rose, beside the more ample presence and accentuated colouring of her friend. 'How kind of you, dear Lady Darlington.'

'Don't you think,' said the latter, 'now you are married you might call me Nina. It is more comfortable.'

Dorothy, with a little show of reluctance, yielded to her wishes, and as they sat familiarly on the same sofa there seemed every prospect of a fine flow of confidences. Contrary, however, to Lady Darlington's expectations, which, womanlike, had soared high in anticipation of some food for gossip, no confidences were offered. Dorothy talked freely of the pictures, of the hot weather, of Venetian life, of trips to be taken in company to the Lido and other picturesque spots, asking many questions about her home, her mother and sister, the Vicar and his wife, and local affairs, but saying not a word of her own inmost feelings or of her matrimonial imbroglios. Lady Darlington dared not ask or seek information. It would clearly have been disobeying her husband's injunctions ; she therefore experienced a decided ebb and check in her eager curiosity.

'What do you do with yourself all the afternoon?' she said presently.

'I stay at home, read or write, or sleep

while it is very hot. Then we go out in our gondola, Keith and I, or Mr. Palis, till dinner-time, and again in the evening.'

'You must pass a good many hours alone?'

'Yes,' said Dorothy ; 'it is unavoidable, I suppose, when one is married. I suffered from the solitude at first, having had mamma or Margaret always at my elbow in old days. But it has its advantages, too. I read a good deal now ; I have taken up my studies again.'

'I see a big, well-worn book there in your work-basket. What is it? Though I scarcely know why I ask, for even if you tell me, I shall be as wise as I was before. I never read a *stiff* book in my life—can't even understand how anyone can.'

Dorothy drew the book from beneath her embroidery.

'It is "Peines et Délits," by Beccaria,' she said, holding it up for her friend's inspection.

'What a dry thing! What is it all about?'

'It is a treatise on crime and its punishment. Beccaria is the great authority for such things, I believe. I found the book on an old bookstall, which accounts for its ugly appearance. You see, I try to improve my French.'

'Why not read French novels? Have you none?'

'Plenty!' Dorothy laughed. 'Keith reads nothing else. See, here they all are: with long names and short names, and every variety of title—all kinds and sorts, nice and nasty, I believe. I am tired of seeing all those yellow-covered volumes lying about, for I don't care for novels; they don't interest me—since I have *lived* one,' she added, with a mysterious smile; 'serious books suit me much better, and send me to sleep too, if necessary.'

'But *crime*—what interest can crime have for *you?*' persisted Lady Darlington.

'Oh, a great deal,' said Dorothy airily. 'I always thought criminals interesting, and liked to read about them—don't you?'

'No; crime is such a vulgar thing.'

'All crimes are not—political crimes, for instance, or those that spring from revenge, love, jealousy.'

'I presume I am not poetical!' said Lady Darlington, smoothing out the frills of her gown. 'I decidedly prefer a quiet humdrum existence to any amount of romance; but you were always high-strung. Dorothy, do you remember I warned you when you were engaged, and told you how to keep your husband's heart ?'

'I remember — by good dinners ! But I have had no chance of putting your advice in practice. Keith had already such an excellent cook, and a treasure in le Goui; and Mr. Palis understands the culinary science to perfection. There is no room for my talents.'

'What *is* Mr. Palis ?' said her friend.

'A journalist—a poet—a man of the world —everything, I think, in turn, but nothing long. He told me himself the violent friendships he takes up never last more than two months.'

'Is it a violent friendship for Mr. Chester ? and has he much influence over him ?'

Lady Darlington felt she could safely satisfy her curiosity on these minor points without disobeying her lord.

'No; they are old, but very *calm*, friends. Keith likes and admires him ; you see, he has always been accustomed to bright and gay society.'

'Ah, my dear !' said Lady Darlington, with a profound air of knowledge ; 'I always distrust men who have apparently nothing on earth to do but to trot about after one's husband and humour all his whims—*creepers,*

I call them — nasty, cringing, wriggling things; they always end by becoming a woman's lover or her enemy.'

'You quite misjudge Mr. Palis,' said Dorothy gaily; 'he could never be either. He is too simple, and too indolent.'

'Simplicity, and a journalist! Be sure, my dear, that is all put on for your edification. Besides, he is half a foreigner, and too fond of onions and garlic.'

'That is true; but he likes sugar-plums, too—chocolate especially.'

'I don't understand the creature'—Lady Darlington shook her head dolefully—'and I don't want to. My advice is, get rid of him, my dear.'

'And order dinner myself, is that it?' said Dorothy, now fairly brimming over with hilarity.

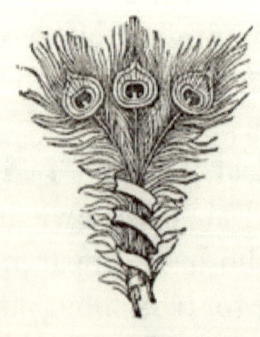

CHAPTER XIV.

COUNT PINSUTI ASSERTS HIMSELF.

LORD DARLINGTON did not share his wife's disparaging opinion of Palis. The latter possessed in a high degree that quality, rare indeed, but essential to a diplomat, or one who aspires to be a leader of men, and the absence of which embitters and endangers friendship— that quality, of so intangible and subtle a character as to defy definition, which only takes root in intensely imaginative and sensitive minds — Palis possessed *tact*. He understood how to suit his conversation as neatly to his company as the Florentine cabinet-maker does the woods of various tints and textures which he fits together to compose a table, or some ingenious and beautiful piece of handiwork.

Palis judged people rapidly at a glance; he seized the salient features of their character correctly, and his sentiments took their cue from the prevailing hue of his associates' thoughts; in the presence of quiet people of somewhat obtuse intelligence, crushing his too vivacious manners, his exuberance of spirits, toning himself down into a subdued gentility, relieved by the faintest spice of natural malice, sufficient to give a sparkle and zest to the conversation.

Lord Darlington was a simple straightforward country gentleman; he loved horses. Palis talked of horses, though, to save his life, he would not have dared seize one by the bridle, preferring always to avail himself of a seat in a lumbering and safe barouche, in company with old or young ladies (young preferred). Yet, in the course of his miscellaneous reading and 'getting up' of journalistic subjects, he had stumbled upon sundry bits of recondite knowledge about horseflesh, which he now aired for Lord Darlington's edification. He discoursed copiously on the breed of Arabs, showed acquaintance with their special points and peculiarities, and knew which was the true strain of blood.

Lord Darlington warmed visibly, offered

the speaker a cigar, took one himself, and said he had long thought of importing some Arab mares, but believed it did not answer.

'You cannot get them — at least, not the best,' said Palis knowingly; 'the Sheikhs will not part with anything really valuable: money will not tempt them.'

'I once had a steeple-chase mare,' said Lord Darlington, 'who was bought by the Egyptian Government to run a race of endurance with Arabs. The distance was eighty miles, and she was ridden by an English lad, too. She beat them all; and yet she was not a wonderful animal, by any means—a stayer, certainly, but she had no speed; that does not say much for the Arab horses, does it? when the English mare beat them on their own sand, under their own sweltering sun. The English horses are the finest in the world. Austrian and Prussian horses are as soft as butter. Percherons can't do fast work, and Arabs have no shoulders.'

'No doubt of it,' said Palis enthusiastically.

'My dear fellow, come down and stay with me in December, at Lovemere Hall, and *I'll* give you a mount worth the finest Arab in the world, on such a splendid animal as, I'll be bound, you've never crossed. I bought him

in Ireland—that's the country for horses ! His
dam ran in the Derby; and I'm having him
broken in now for her ladyship to hunt next
winter.'

Palis accepted this offer of hospitality with
outward glee, inwardly registering a vow that
nothing should tempt him in the depths of a
chilly winter to go within miles of a place
where the inmates talked of nothing but sport,
and the very women rode to hounds.

Presently Lord Darlington, suddenly recalled to a sense of the object of their expedition, which he had momentarily forgotten in
the delights of horsey talk, put a few leading
questions respecting the Marchesa to his companion.

'Is she really handsome?—does Chester
admire her ?'

'She is a splendid woman !' emphasized
Palis, throwing his dimpled short-fingered
hands about expressively (he loved dark and
joyous beauties). 'Charming, unscrupulous,
plays the piano delightfully ; but I don't
think cares a fig for Keith—or, indeed, for
anyone except herself !'

'Excellent ! I am afraid Keith is a flirt?'

'By habit only. By nature he is cold—a
sluggish circulation. I believe him to be

devoted to his charming wife, in his own
peculiar indolent and "grand seigneur"
fashion. He ought to have been a King
Ahasuerus, and he would have held out the
golden sceptre to Esther with becoming
dignity !'

'Do you think he gives himself airs ?'

'No, no! You don't understand me.' Palis
lowered his voice and became confidential,
patting the cushions rhythmically with his little
fat hands. 'The airs I speak of are innate—
he is unconscious of them. He is naturally
haughty, contemptuous, cynical by tempera-
ment, but so exquisitely refined, and has such perfect manners, that he only appears superlatively
and un-Englishly polite. The English are not
very polished, you know,' he added apolo-
getically.

'We don't make phrases,' said Lord Darlington. 'Thank God for that! I hate
palaver. But if you want a downright honest
friend, the true Briton is your man. He might
not step into the gutter and raise his hat whenever he meets a woman he does not know, to
oblige her ; but he will stick up for an absent
"pal" behind his back, and remain your
friend through thick and thin.'

'Certainly. *My* best friend is an English-

13—2

man. Do you know him — Hugh Vennaker ?'

'I haven't the pleasure of his acquaintance. Is he in your line of life ? Literature, isn't it ?'

'No, he can't scribble a bit. Besides, he's the eldest son of a very rich man ; but he goes in for music. Plays the piano—has a touch like Chopin!—and sings delightfully. A splendid fellow! He would come up to my room this summer straight from the river in his flannels and play the piano, just as he was, till we forgot all about the dinner-hour.'

'Ah !' said Lord Darlington, who was not a bit musical ; 'but you're fond of your dinner, ain't you? Know all about it, too, in a kind of connoisseur way, don't you? I should prefer your friend if he hunted.'

'I dare say he does ; he rides, I know. We intend to set up house together, when we return. His father keeps him very tight ; but that won't signify—we shall be very happy !'

'Exactly,' said Lord Darlington, whom this domestic talk about a stranger now slightly bored ; puffing in the direction of the canal, he added : 'Are we near ?'

His new friend, quick as thought, changed the venue, and rattled off on a new subject.

While the two men thus discoursed, other events were taking place in the Marchesa's palace. At an early hour of the afternoon, and previous to Keith's arrival, Count Pinsuti had asked an audience of the Marchesa. She, Sultana-like, replied that he might wait; which he accordingly did. The lady's prime principles, in her dealings with men, being that they must never be treated like kings, but like slaves—slavish adoration being the natural outcome of unreasoning worship—and men, as a rule, bore out the truth of her philosophy by humbly cringing at her feet, and gratefully receiving any stray favours she might chance to fling to them. The favours being pretty impartially distributed, the charm of rarity and doubt was thus added to their value.

The Count had for some time enjoyed a more or less undisputed monopoly in the share of her smiles ; that is to say, according to her arbitrary valuation. He fetched and carried more than anyone else, waited more patiently, obeyed more implicitly, admired more earnestly, and consequently was doubly appreciated. All this, however, dated from the prehistoric period—before Keith's advent.

Since then the Count had been snubbed,

set aside, contemned, almost brutally driven away. With the stubborn endurance of a narrow and ignorant mind he waited—at first patiently, then impatiently, but always silently —until he finally decided that an explanation must take place this very day. The Marchesa was welcome to treat him badly, but she should treat no one better ; she might frown upon him, but she must not smile upon another ; she might depress, degrade, humiliate him, but she should *not* exalt another, especially when that other was a married man, on whom all the gifts of fickle fortune had already been showered.

Thus decided within himself the Count of the ape-like face, the old and honoured title, and the sly and cunning disposition. He himself could have married any day a wife from among the best families in Venice ; but he preferred to remain single and dally with the Marchesa ; and he scornfully rejected the idea of yielding an iota of one of his hardly-earned rights.

The Marchesa, at her toilette, sitting in front of her mirror, gazing with admiration at her long silky hair with the blue sheen gleaming in its ebony depths, smiling at the reflection of her handsome face, and debating whether she

would wear a tawny yellow or a creamy white
robe on this afternoon, knew nothing of the
Count's strange aberrations. Lapped in the
lazy luxury of her own fancies, she had neither
perceived the Count's pique, his smothered
rage, nor his final boiling up of despair ; indeed, it is doubtful whether in any case she
would have condescended to notice it, for she
was a very great lady—and great ladies are
not easily put out by the strength of other
people's feelings.

Her husband was absent at the tiresome
country-seat where she was always so extremely bored. He was happy superintending
the harvest, the olive-yards, the tree-planting,
drilling dull peasants, and hearing the evening
croaking of frogs. *She* was alone in Venice ;
and she saw Keith every day. The mind of
the Marchesa (but would it not be flattery
to call that a mind, which was only a chaotic
mass of selfish desires, purely personal aspi-
rations, languid enjoyments, vanities, puny
conceits and vacuity?) was set upon enchaining
Keith, and displaying him as a captive attached
to her triumphal car ; and further, upon
estranging him completely from the innocent
and gentle woman who (her rival was forced

unwillingly to confess it) still reigned supreme over his affections.

Hitherto, the Marchesa scarcely dared hope she had made any definite impression upon Mr. Chester; he still conversed as unconcernedly as on the occasion of his first visit to her; still played his violin; still drank his tea, or sipped iced lemonade, with the air of a man perfectly at home and indifferent; and though spending much of his time in her company, she could construe none of his bantering talk and graceful compliments into the semblance of a tender sentiment, or anything but the pleasant intercourse of two musical enthusiasts.

'How I could ever have let him go,' she said to herself reproachfully, 'when he was last in Venice and we were friends, without finding out half the charm he has for me—that it should have been reserved for me to know this only when he was married to a pretty baby—is incomprehensible to me. Fool that I have been !'

The Marchesa, whose *coiffure* was completed to the satisfaction of herself and her bright-eyed Italian maid, now decided upon the tawny yellow costume, and leisurely descended to the *salon*, where the Count had already impatiently waited for about three-quarters of an hour.

The process of waiting when you have something disagreeable to say, that you are anxious to get said and done with, is not one likely to cool an ardent lover's anger and jealousy; and the Count was by this time stewing and choking with rage, and more determined than ever to provoke a decisive explosion.

'Count! Good-morning! I am afraid I have kept you waiting a little,' she said, sailing in unconcernedly, and looking more gracious and fascinating than ever.

'You *always* keep me waiting; and if it is your good-pleasure, I do not complain,' said he, bowing low over her hand ; 'but there are *other* things of which I complain.'

'The heat of the weather, perhaps?' she said haughtily, interrupting him; 'you should go *en villegiature.* The Marquis writes that the country is charming, but even if it is hot, you need not complain of the heat—a wise man bears inevitable ills in silence.'

'If they *are* inevitable!'

'What do you mean?' she said coldly, seating herself. 'Why do you talk in riddles? *You* have nothing to complain of, I am sure!'

'You do understand, then, that I wish to

complain?' he said, taking a chair near her, and looking earnestly and firmly into her face.

'Of what?' she said languidly, examining her slim fingers, the diamond rings on which sent sparkling rainbow flashes across to where he sat.

'Of you!' he said hotly; 'of you, whom I adore.'

'If I don't adore you, what possible right does that give you to complain? I don't quite see the drift of your remark,' she said pointedly, dropping out her words with carefully adjusted deliberation and indifference.

'You loved me once!'

'Never!' she said more quickly, though still preserving the same cold and equable tone.

'Before that man—that idiotic Englishman came,' he persisted, 'you loved me! I came and went as I liked—you encouraged me—I was necessary to you!'

'You come and go now, it seems, Count,' she said, in a more cutting tone, smoothing out some folds of her gown with suppressed irritation, 'whenever the spirit prompts you. You were here this morning before I was even dressed!'

'And you made me wait. I waited.'

'Of course! What else would you have? That is what you came for, I suppose?'

'Listen, Madame la Marquise'—the little Count's voice trembled; he rose hastily and perambulated the room with crisp quarter-deck steps—'I *will* be *first* in your affections! I was so once.'

'And if I *will* not, sir, my will is as strong as yours, I am convinced; let us talk of something else.'

'No—no! You always put me off with excuses, you *shall* hear me out! I have *proved* my devotion to you; I *demand* my reward! Send away the Englishman, and let all the past be forgotten; we will live again in a new and brighter future.'

'I shall not send away the Englishman. Who will play the violin to me?' she said firmly, ignoring the rest of his peroration.

'Then *I* will!' answered the little Count, his eyes sparkling, and his diminutive ugly appearance gaining a kind of dignity from this resolve. 'If need be I shall *kill* him; and he may learn what is the vengeance of an Italian!'

The Marchesa kept silence, and looked with dismay at the speaker. He was small, but

he was sharp and cunning : a midnight
vengeance—a stab in the back—truly such a
contingency was possible.

'You would not really carry out your
threat?' she said persuasively; 'I know you
only say this to frighten me.'

'I say what I mean. My love for you is
very serious, madame, and not to be trifled
with!'

'But, Count, be reasonable. Sit down; listen.'

The Count turned his head to listen, but he
did not sit down.

'Let us be the very best of friends. You
shall come here whenever you like: will that
satisfy you?'

'Yes, if you send the Englishman away.'

The Count subtly surmised that, his rival
once fairly out of the way, the path would lie
clear for him to urge his suit.

'He will go soon,' she said, in a distinct
voice ; 'he must return to his own country.
Why should I quarrel with him?'

'Marchesa, you can choose; I have said my
say.'

The Marchesa threw him a swift look of
hatred; and the door at that instant opened
and admitted Mr. Chester.

Count Pinsuti immediately rose; and after

the customary greeting, into which he infused
a satirically exaggerated politeness, he took
his leave, saying in a warning voice to the
Marchesa, as he did so :

' I shall return later to receive any orders
you may have to give me, madame.'

The Marchesa bowed her head slightly, but
did not speak for some moments, during
which she leant back in her chair, gloomily
contemplating her small slippered foot. She
was taking a resolution; the crisis had come
upon her sooner than she anticipated. The
Count, on whom she had proudly trodden,
worm-like had turned; he must be crushed at
once, and for that she needed an ally. To
secure the ally she needed reflection.

Keith, on his side, cool, gentlemanly, and
pleasantly amused, seated himself in his accustomed place to await the lady's good pleasure,
unconsciously fingering a cut-glass phial containing eau-de-Cologne, which lay on the small
gold console beside him.

The silence lasted a while. These two were
intimate enough now to understand and appreciate silence. At last the Marchesa roused
herself. Possibly she had decided upon her
course of action ; the resolution was taken.

' Mr. Chester,' she said slowly, ' don't you

think the Count has become very tiresome? I am in a bad temper to-day. The sirocco is in the air, perhaps, or I am more sensitive than usual, but it gets on my nerves. What is one to do when that happens to one with an acquaintance?'

'It is difficult to say. Drop the acquaintance quietly, I suppose.'

'Impossible!' The Marchesa made a gesture of despair.

'Then be firm and determined; decline to receive his visits.'

'Impossible!' again said the Marchesa despondingly.

'What is to be done then? Tolerate him?'

'Impossible! He will not be tolerated,' she said in a low voice.

'Ma foi! What can I advise?'

'Yet you alone can advise me. I believe you to be my sincere friend.'

Keith's eyes answered:

'Certainly.'

'You do not know how often I need a real friend.'

Keith looked sympathetic.

'I thought——' She stopped, and treated him to a glance from her fine languorous eyes, in whose depths he could read passion and

entreaty. 'I thought——' she resumed with
an apparent effort; then suddenly: 'Oh, Mr.
Chester, I am so lonely!'

She buried her face in her hands and burst
into tears.

So proud a woman in tears! It affected
Keith somewhat, though at that moment he
knew with certainty that it was only compassion, and no tenderer sentiment, moving
him to take her limp hanging hand, and
whisper in her ear:

'Calm yourself, my dear Marchesa.'

'I will, if you tell me,' she murmured low,
letting her fingers close round his.

The situation was somewhat embarrassing.
The Marchesa's bosom still heaved with sobs,
tears streamed from her eyes, which she
stanched with the delicate cambric handkerchief she held in one hand, while the other
clasped Keith's fingers. How is it possible
to console a pretty woman, except by assuring
her of your love? And to such a declaration
Keith did not feel inclined to commit himself.
So he said nothing, feeling intensely clumsy;
and the Marchesa found nothing better to do
than gradually to dry her tears and withdraw
her hand from his.

'I have behaved like a fool and a brute to

the poor woman,' thought Keith, while yet
rejoicing to escape further complications.

'I am absurdly weak and emotional,' she
said, looking at him with a mournful air.
'It must be the weather. Do not mind my
tears.'

'I *do* mind them,' said Keith. 'I cannot
endure to see a charming woman in trouble.
Believe me, I am *very* sorry for you. Shall
we play something to distract you—or what
can I do?'

The Marchesa sighed. Perhaps she thought
further confidences were due to her from
Keith ; perhaps she thought the little drama
she had played had not resulted in success.
Suffice it, that after the lapse of a few awkward
moments, the pair were not sorry when Palis
and Lord Darlington were announced.

Keith, without any show of reluctance,
ceded his place to Lord Darlington, who at
once decided in his own mind that the
Marchesa was a far handsomer woman than
rumour had led him to anticipate. Her recent
tears had given unwonted softness to her
sphinx-like eyes ; her soft and creamy skin
had lost none of its delicacy of tone, and her
manner was more sweetly sympathetic than
ever.

Keith conversed in the embrasure of the window with Palis, who, while pretending to notice nothing, registered the moral certitude that he and Lord Darlington had interrupted a passionate love-scene.

Things soon resumed their normal aspect, but Keith carefully avoided lingering behind. When the English lord's visit had arrived at a conventional length the three men took their departure together.

'Which way are we going now?' said Lord Darlington, looking at his watch, as they stood on the marble steps near the gaily-striped post to which the gondola was attached. 'I am getting hungry. By Jove! that *is* a handsome woman, for a foreigner. Does she paint?'

CHAPTER XV.

JOYNTE AGAIN.

AT the farther end of an alley bordered with small shops, chiefly for jewellery, in which the fine gold chains for which Venice is famous were displayed, dressed in a plain morning-gown of blue and white linen, and wearing a broadbrimmed straw hat, garnished with a wreath of wild-flowers, stood Dorothy in front of a bookstall absorbed in the silent perusal of a book which she had taken up, and was holding in her hand while she read it. Here Joynte found her. He had approached so close to her that he could have touched her shoulder or whispered in her ear. He even became conscious of a certain sweet smell of heliotrope that hung about her garments, but as yet she had neither heard nor seen him. Her book engrossed her entirely.

'Mrs. Chester,' he said at last.

She started at the sound of his voice. It had come then—the meeting she had so dreaded, that for days she dared not venture out alone; now, just as her terror had begun to diminish, the monster stood again at her elbow, like a second Mephistopheles, trying to sow the seeds of suspicion and of guilty imaginings within her heart. She had succeeded, after some effort, in driving from her mind the vivid recollection of Joynte's threats; she had dispelled her own doubts; she disbelieved his accusations; she had confidently established, to her own satisfaction, by a long course of reasoning, the utter fallacy of any unpleasant mysteries. Only a lurking jealousy of the Marchesa, which she strove against courageously, still disturbed the equanimity of her happiness; and behold, just when her confidence, and innocent security, returned to her, this man must needs shatter the whole fabric. She looked at Joynte with wide-open terrified eyes—the eyes of one who tries to avoid the inevitable; she looked up the street and down again for a mode of escape, but her tongue was paralyzed.

'Well, Mrs. Chester, you didn't expect to
see me again, did you?' said the American
jauntily, perceiving his advantage and warming to the work. 'I warned you how it
would be. If you remember, I told you you
had not seen the last of me. Suppose now
you drop your grand airs, my lady, and listen
to me—come!'

Joynte was not quite comfortable in this
gentlewoman's presence; she awed him in
spite of his bravado.

'What do you want?' she said softly, bowing her head.

'Well,' he said, with a laugh, 'I guess I
want a great deal more money than the last
time, my lady. I've gone up in value, it
seems; and yet I've gone down in the world.'

Dorothy silently glanced at his shabby
dress and miserable appearance.

'Down in the world, you see, a bit more
than I was; that's the way of it. One goes
up, and another down; I guess that makes it
all square. Now, listen—I'm not given to fine
words. You and Mr. Chester want your secret
kept : name your price. I'll engage not to
trouble you for £1,000, though I'll take more
if you like to offer it. I can't do it for less;
every chap must look out for himself.'

'I don't know what you mean,' she said, in a cold clear voice, moving on a little in the direction of home. 'I have already told you that I wish you would settle your affairs with Mr. Chester ; I know nothing about his business matters !'

'No!' he said, with a sly and cruel look ; 'perhaps it would be better for you if you did. Maybe you never heard tell how your husband got his money?'

'I have heard it was left to him;' she drew herself up proudly.

'Under what circumstances?'

'You have no right to annoy me in this way here, in the public streets!' she said nervously; 'if you do not leave me at once I will call for assistance!'

'Pray do. There are plenty of people about; but you will repent the scandal far more than I shall. I have *nothing* to lose, you have *everything*—position, fortune, an adored husband!'

Joynte had learnt his lesson well. Here, in the company of this young and delicate creature, he felt no fear.

Dorothy shrank within herself; it was true she knew nothing. Who could tell what harm might come of too hasty an action on her part? Joynte pursued, quickening his pace to keep up with her.

'Mr. Chester's money was left to him by a woman whom he cruelly injured; and——'

'I don't wish to hear blame of my husband,' interrupted Dorothy. 'Have you anything else to say?'

'You are right; perhaps I have no business to soil your virtuous ears with ugly stories;' his tone was insufferably sarcastic. 'Suffice it, then, that your husband is a criminal, and that I must have hush-money. Do you understand?'

'I understand nothing, except that you wish to frighten me into giving you money,' she said firmly. 'What is your address? Why should there be any mystery about you? Why not come to our house, and speak to Mr. Chester in my presence?'

'Because he will choose to run the risk of detection sooner than to pay my just demands; but I am desperate now. Besides, you yourself, with that fair proud face, would turn from him with loathing if you knew all.'

'Never!' said Dorothy quickly.

'You are very bold, my lady; but the time will come, very soon maybe, when you will not be so bold.'

'I will speak to my husband about you,' she said, with a touch of pity for the miscreant in her voice. 'I will ask him to give you money, but I can do nothing for you myself.'

'Will you now—do you mean it?' says Joynte eagerly; then, checking his impulse of joy, 'Mind you do now, or it will be the worse for you; I'm a desperate man.'

'I don't know what Mr. Chester will say— I don't know if he will help you; but if he *has* injured you (unwittingly I am sure), if you *have* any claim upon him, I shall use all my efforts to urge him to make reparation.'

'He has injured me. Look at me, if you don't believe what I say. *I*, who was once a gentleman——'

The beggarly whine, with the true professional mendicant ring about it, with which he uttered these words, stifled the momentary spark of pity in her breast. She continued coldly:

'I can promise nothing, except that if it is *justice* you want, you shall have it, as far as it lies in my power.'

'When shall I hear from you?'

'Give me your address.'

'No, indeed, and be nabbed like a fox in his lair! No, my lady; I'll meet you *here* whenever you like—that's the best arrangement.'

'Here, then, on Tuesday next,' said Dorothy, after an instant's hesitation. 'Leave me now.'

'You may count on my discretion,' he answered with a lofty bow, almost pathetic in its absurdity.

Dorothy hurried on, casting no look behind her, as Joynte disappeared into a neighbouring alley. She was already late for breakfast, and her head was in a turmoil. Soon she would know everything and be released from this thick cloud of mystery and terror that hung about her and poisoned her very life. Soon she would be mistress of Keith's secrets, and discover that he was worthy of her trust. With a lighter heart she pursued her way, hailing the hour that was to bring a blessed certainty, instead of the gnawing uncertainty in which she lived.

CHAPTER XVI.

FEMININE CONFIDENCES.

DOROTHY, however, found no immediate opportunity of speaking to
her husband. He came in after
they had sat down to breakfast,
talked little, eat less, and seemed considerably
preoccupied. Directly after the meal he
again disappeared; and Lady Darlington
arrived, more cheery and chatty than ever, to
fetch her friend. She had shifted the burden
of her care about Dorothy's trouble on to her
husband's broad shoulders, and with the happy
trust that formed one of the principal in-
gredients in the harmony of their conjugal
arrangements, she felt herself free to devote
her time quietly to sight-seeing and gossiping.
She was sustained by a never-flagging curiosity

and a childlike interest in the shifting scenes
and the strange habits of the people, which
had the power to amuse her infinitely more
than pictures, by however great a master,
about which she understood nothing, and
marble churches for which she cared less.
She needed Mrs. Chester's society at all times;
she liked her to share her simple pleasures
and all her sensations of wonder and admiration. She would come running in like a stray
sunbeam or a small whirlwind every morning,
and cry encouragingly:

'Do come out, Dorothy! Never mind the
heat; it's nothing if you don't think about it,
and wear a veil. Darlington has gone off
with your husband somewhere, and I have
seen such a funny place which I am dying to
explore with you.'

Dorothy would smile in return, shut up
her book or fold her work, and sally out with
her friend, patiently following her lead into all
kinds of odd corners and out-of-the-way places,
explaining and expatiating whenever possible,
by the aid of her superior knowledge. It
happened consequently that for several days
Dorothy could obtain no moments of intimate
talk with her husband. They were never
alone until late in the evening, when Keith

complained of sleepiness and fatigue, and she instinctively felt it would not be a propitious moment for so serious an explanation. Strange to say, though she believed that the hour which was to bring her a pleasant certainty had only been deferred, she could not divest herself of a nervous and unreasonable anxiety, which clouded her brow, disturbed her slumbers, and kept her quieter and sadder than usual. The few days of respite Joynte had allowed her were now nearly expired. Monday morning dawned, and on Tuesday she had promised to meet him. Human nature, weak and erring, shrinks from the foretaste of pain; it is easier to say to ourselves, 'I *can* know, when I like,' than to stretch out our hand for the knowledge which may bring with it fresh responsibilities and greater difficulties.

Throughout the relations between herself and her husband, there had existed a one-sided state of things, owing certainly to her own mistaken delicacy and ignorance of the world, but still much to be deplored. She had lavished upon Keith all the devotion of which she was capable, and she had checked his wiser efforts to confide his faults to her. Consequently a barrier of mental reserve lay between them which increased her present difficulty.

How was she to speak to him of any subject which nearly concerned his own private affairs, and about which her questions might seem a mark of suspicion and interference?

Only once had the cloud of reserve between them been fairly dispelled, and that was on the occasion of her jealous outburst after the ball; an outburst she had regretted and repented of ever since, as an act of disloyalty towards her husband.

Keith noticed none of these mental struggles. He kissed his wife affectionately and carelessly morning and night, and escorted her occasionally on some of the expeditions which she made in the company of her English friends—picnics, al-fresco dinners, suppers, or musical evenings on the water, but there was no question of mutual confidence between them.

The eventful interview with the Marchesa, which Lord Darlington and Palis interrupted, has been recorded; it afforded Keith considerable food for rumination. He had behaved unfeelingly towards the poor lady, he was afraid, at a time when she was already deprived of sympathy and affection in her own home, and sought it in the society of intimate friends, thinking no harm. He had been a fool, and a prig. Keith's vanity whispered to him, that for a pretty woman to give him her confidence was the finest compliment she could pay him. Keith's common-sense urged, that perhaps, after all, he had mistaken her meaning, and that her words and looks could bear the most unstrained and innocent interpretation. Then Keith, easy in his vanity, fell to hoping that the latter hypothesis were not the true one; finally thought it necessary to assure himself of the fact, and to make his visits to the Marchesa considerably more frequent. She, with the wiliness of a coquette, now read all his thoughts, and played with him accordingly. Alternately mocking and gay, or sad and sentimental, making little returns upon herself of sorrow and pretty self-upbraidings, she pricked, and piqued, and maddened him beyond endurance. To himself he said comfortably:

'I do not care for her in the least, but it is an experience.'

The Marchesa knew better. She knew that she was gradually gaining a mastery over this man, which would make him her slave just for so long as she chose to keep him.

On this very Monday, when Dorothy kept saying to herself reproachfully, 'I *must*, I really *must* speak to Keith about that poor man to-day!' the Marchesa organized another little explosion. Count Pinsuti had been making himself intensely disagreeable, as indeed was his habit; had muttered darkly of revenge, and a determination to stand *it* no longer; the *it* vaguely hinted at being painfully clear to the Marchesa's experience. She, on her part, thought fit to bring matters between herself and Mr. Chester to a crisis. When he arrived, violin in hand, at the usual time—which was now accelerated by at least an hour—he found her grave and silent, with the air of some one who has come to a serious determination. This in itself annoyed him. When a man lets himself drift, he cannot bear to be brought up sharply by the checks of another's resolution. Having exchanged morning greetings, he ventured to ask if she were indisposed, or had any cause for sorrow.

'None that *you* would understand,' was the reply. 'I am going to the country.'

'Indeed!' Keith's countenance fell. 'Is not this a sudden resolve?'

'It is one I think necessary,' she said drily.

'When do you go?'

'That depends. To-morrow or the next day, perhaps.'

'And, in that case, I shall not be able to

come and see you every day ; and music will
be at a standstill, now it has become the delightful habit of my present life. How I shall
miss you!'

'I don't think so,' she said gravely, avoiding
all coquettish airs and graces. 'You will
equally have the society of Lord and Lady
Darlington, and of Mr. Palis, and—your
wife!' She dropped her voice at the end of
the sentence.

'But I *shall* miss you!' he said warmly.

'That is a mere phrase,' she answered,
shrugging her shoulders. 'One only misses
what is absolutely necessary to one's happiness. Unfortunately, I have tasted of the
realities of life, and I have learnt to despise
mere conversational froth.'

'My words were not conversational froth!'

Her contemptuous tone irritated Keith exceedingly.

'Were they not?' she said, a little more
coldly. 'Do not let us dispute; I dare say
the country will be charming.'

'Am I never to see you, then?'

'Oh yes! when I return, if you are still
here—in a couple of months, perhaps.'

'And until then——' his voice was filled
with regret.

'Until then, I suppose, you will exist pretty much as you have done hitherto; you will continue to behave as the model husband —the kind friend.'

'Why do you taunt me in this way?' he said sharply.

'I? Don't you always speak with the utmost veneration of your wife's perfections? are you not devoted to one another? am I not right to take the cue from your own lips——'

'Let my wife alone, please,' he interrupted harshly; 'she has nothing whatever to do in this discussion.'

'Ah, there it is, you see!' said the Marchesa, leaning back in her chair, and beginning to play with her bracelets. 'How can I, a lonely, neglected creature, talk happily and unconcernedly, as does the woman you love? Sometimes—don't be shocked—sometimes I envy her dreadfully. Why should she have had all the chances? If you had loved *me*, I should have been as good, as innocent, as pure — innocence is only ignorance, after all; a mere matter of education. Don't you think *I* have the makings in me of a good and devoted wife?—of course. I have a heart, intellect—all the instincts of self-devotion—

and yet I am tied to a boor, who neglects me
—whom I was not even allowed to choose for
myself, but was *sold* to when a mere child.
Ah! why is life so unequal in its chances? why
is Heaven so unjust? why has your wife *every-*
thing that woman can desire, and I *nothing*—
nothing that I hunger for? My heart is
empty—no one loves me.'

'You are mistaken, Marchesa; everyone
loves you—Count Pinsuti adores you.'

'He — that wretched little object? He
bores me. A woman cannot express greater
indifference to a man than by saying that he
bores her.'

'Do *I* bore you?' he said, without thought,
his eager vanity asserting itself imperiously.

'You?'

In that one little word the Marchesa bared
her heart, her wishes, her intentions—in that
one word she made her declaration—in that
one word Keith read everything, and struck
the full chords of her envy, her jealousy,
her restless desires. He rose hastily: something within him seemed to whisper, 'Fly—
fly, while it is yet time.' He was no paragon
of virtue, certainly; but he remembered his
gentle wife at home. He was no knight *sans*
peur et sans reproche; the cynicism of his

own maxims of life had blended with the coldness of his heart and disregard of principle : yet even worldly prudence warned him to take care.

' Don't go !' The Marchesa had comprehended his movement, and sprang up herself to arrest him. ' Once before you left me sad and unhappy; speak to me now — comfort me.'

She was standing beside him, the fire of her large eyes seeming to burn into his brain, and confuse his reason with doubt, fear, inclination, and vanity, mixed in one strange medley.

' Keith !' She threw an unutterable tenderness into her voice. The woman was an accomplished actress, and on this occasion she was scarcely acting. Her lips shaped themselves into words of love, and her eyes followed suit. He made a step backwards, and seized her hand in both of his. ' You will come again ?' she said earnestly, looking at him with her passionate eyes. He bowed his head, and hastily left the room.

Even Lady Darlington noticed Keith's strange preoccupation at dinner that evening; his absence of mind; the irrelevant answers he gave to questions, to which they had no possible reference; the way that he poured water into a glass, and forgot he had done so, and then went on pouring in more water, till the liquid ran over upon the cloth; his silence, and his evident anxiety to escape from his friends. And all this time Dorothy was waiting for a convenient opportunity to begin the interview, which *must* be gone through with to-night.

After dinner, Keith retired to his library, ostensibly to write letters. Lady Darlington began to play the piano in the saloon, trying with one finger to pick out the melody of Palis's favourite song; the latter smoked and talked with Lord Darlington on the balcony.

Dorothy, spying her chance, quick as thought slipped from the room and followed her husband. She found him sitting at the carved bureau, in his large leather armchair, with the silver inkstand of best Florentine style in front of him, and some papers spread all about. But she could see that he was not writing—only idly making little blots and figures on the spotless paper with his pen. She stole softly near, and laid her hand on his shoulder. He started violently.

'Keith, I want to speak to you.'

'What is it? Don't you see I am busy?'

He drew another sheet of paper towards
him, and tried to appear as if he were lost in
abstruse calculations.

'Oh, Keith, spare me an instant, and don't
be angry, dear!' She slid down on her
knees, and laid her arm on his chair. He did
not encourage her or help her one little bit;
but the humble, pleading attitude seemed
to aid her in her difficult explanation. 'I
met a man,' she continued, hesitatingly jerk-
ing out her words, 'two or three days ago,
who knows you. He spoke to me, and said
many things I could not understand.' Still
he gave her no sign of approval, and only
bent a little forward, as if about to dip his
pen in the ink. 'You know, Keith, I have
never asked you one single question that
might seem to imply a want of confidence. I
trust you too much for that; but, dear, he
says you have injured him, and I have promised him, for your own sake, to repair this
injustice—if it exists.'

'What is the man's name?'

'Elias F. Joynte.'

Her voice trembled; she dared not think
of the consequences of this revelation. Keith's
face twitched a little, but otherwise he showed
no emotion.

'It is the old story. He tried to set your mother against me, you know--and Dorothy, I forbid you to speak to him. He is mad! I will arrange for him to be locked up.'

'Don't harm him, Keith. Poor creature! I don't believe he is really mad. He talked sensibly enough — said he was a desperate man. Won't you give him the money he asks for? He says if you will do that, he will engage never to trouble you again.'

'The wretch!' growled Keith between his teeth. 'How much does he ask?'

'A thousand pounds.'

'Is that all? Only a thousand pounds! He is very moderate in his demands, upon my word! Tell him to go to Jericho!' he added, with sudden fury—'no, of course you can't—I will tell him myself. Is he here?'

'No; he would not give me his address. Keith, don't be rash. What is it? Do tell me what is his claim upon you?'

She had not meant to say this : she had thought he would confide in her of his own accord ; but now she felt that any further mystery was unendurable. She *must* know all.

'My dear, don't alarm yourself. It is a mere nothing,' said Keith, with a slight laugh, in which she detected more fear than fun.

'He must not be allowed to annoy you in any way. I will speak to the proper authorities. The thing he refers to was a transaction of my bachelor days. But, as I have already told you, he is mad. Leave him to me, dear. I will get rid of him.'

Dorothy still knelt on in her humble attitude, looking out of her troubled eyes, and her anxieties scarcely set at rest by Keith's manner.

'I must see him then,' she said, 'and tell him the result of my mission; for I promised to do this,' she added, no longer timidly, remembering it was her clear duty.

'No; as he is mad, it is not safe. Who knows what he might say or do? Where had you arranged a rendezvous?'

A light shone in her husband's eyes which she did not like. He seemed so wild and strange himself to-night, and in all his words and gestures he had showed no love for her.

'I will not go to him, as you forbid it,' she said, rising from her knees and standing straight and composed before him; 'but I cannot betray the poor man's secret unless I know your intentions towards him.'

'As you please,' he said, a little wearily, turning towards the table.

'Keith—haven't you a word for me?' she cried, flinging her arms round his neck. 'Speak to me—comfort me!'

She used the self-same words that the Marchesa had used that afternoon.

Keith kissed her gently; but his kiss chilled her. There was no love in it. He was thinking that all women were alike—insatiable in their demands upon a man's time and affections.

He wanted as much comfort himself, at that moment, as she did. This reappearance of Joynte's was perplexing; and the worst of it was, he did not quite see the end of it.

Everyone knew, that to give hush-money was to condemn one's self to a lifelong slavery; and still he had not quite the courage to stand it out and face disagreeable consequences.

There was no knowing what might happen. Ida's mother was still alive. He never could have borne to give up his riches now; and besides, what would the world say?

Dorothy slowly unwound her arms from his neck, and went out, sobbing a little quietly to herself. Yes! Keith was certainly changed, terribly, incomprehensibly changed.

CHAPTER XVII.

THE SHADOW OF FORMER DAYS.

KEITH hurried off the next day, at least two hours earlier than usual, to pay a visit to the Marchesa. The latter was of so incomprehensible and capricious a nature that he scarcely knew whether to fear or to hope; scarcely felt certain whether she might not have departed for the country, having merely amused herself at his expense. The handsomest woman in Venice in love with him! Could it be true? And the whole affair had originated entirely in her own impulses, for he himself had never thought of anything but the violin-playing.

Naturally, his vanity was extremely flattered; —and yet it seemed but a kind of Dead Sea fruit after all, the taste of which was bitter in his mouth. The flutter and excitement caused by the Marchesa's conduct sufficed to blind him somewhat to the fact of Dorothy's troubled looks, and to the annoyance of Joynte's reappearance.

'After all,' he said to himself, stepping lightly along, 'after all, it was only at the time of my marriage that he had any power to harm me ; for, certainly, if the old lady had heard his story, she would probably not have believed mine, or have allowed me to marry her daughter ; but now, I really cannot see who would even listen to him.'

Thus comforting himself, Keith prepared his most charming manner, wherewith to greet and captivate the Marchesa. She was at home. She had not left Venice ; and she even assured him that she had decided to defer her journey indefinitely. All his wishes, therefore, were realized. She was wise enough to behave to Mr. Chester much as usual ; to make no further declarations, and to imply nothing but the tenderest of friendships. This behaviour suited his fancy exactly—to hover on the confines of sentiment rather than to plunge into the mazes of passion. He did not object to wear a chain, but it must be a chain of roses ; he had no dislike to spoiling and flattery, as long as emotions of an overwhelming and exhausting nature were carefully consigned to the background.

They spent some agreeable hours together, looking over new music, and trying songs; finding one another's company even more delightful than usual, until Keith, in the very midst of a song, suddenly put his hand to his head.

'What is the matter?' said the Marchesa tenderly, by this time considering herself entitled to a vested right in his sensations.

'A violent pain has just seized me,' he answered. 'I feel giddy—I think I must leave you.'

'Perhaps you walked too quickly in the sun?'

'Possibly.'

'Take great care of yourself,' she continued gently; 'your health is very precious to your friends. I shall send to inquire about you to-night. Meanwhile, my gondola shall take you home. And pray see a doctor as soon as possible.'

Mr. Chester's premature return caused considerable surprise in his own home, where his servants were accustomed to his presence only at meals; but Dorothy, who, looking out of the window, had recognised the Marchesa's gondola, asked no questions.

She had just come from an expedition made in company with Lord and Lady Darlington and Mr. Palis, and they were now sitting round the low table, drinking five o'clock tea.

'Don't let me disturb you,' said Keith, as he passed through the boudoir in which they were assembled. 'I have a headache, and I am going to lie down.'

Declining Dorothy's offers of assistance, he stretched himself on the sofa in his dressing-room, and damping a handkerchief in eau-de-Cologne, he bathed his hot brow.

Was it attributable to indisposition, to giddiness, or was it an unwelcome return of memory? He could swear that he had seen a phantom of the past, just now, on his way home—a figure leaning against a marble pillar beside a porch, changed, saddened, shabbier, but still with the same eyes, reproachful and passionate, the eyes of Judith.

Judith! Why should thoughts of her cling so persistently to his spirit this afternoon? Judith must be dead. She was very ill when last he heard of her in Rome, three years ago. He had not inquired about her since ; he had forgotten her. How, indeed, could she be here ? It must have been a mistake on his part, an hallucination of his sick brain. And yet, even as he pressed the cool and fragrant handkerchief to his burning eyes, the phantom haunted him still. It seemed to enter by the door, to come, with a floating motion, nearer and ever nearer ; to fix its large sad eyes upon him, till their rays pierced into his heart, and bared in all its contemptible folly the poor frivolous ideal of life and duty he had always upheld, to stretch out its hands pleadingly towards him. Then rapidly he saw a fierce, unearthly triumph light up the worn face of the phantom, and Keith felt himself slipping, slipping, being dragged away against his will, whither he knew not, while he frantically and unavailingly grasped at anything within his reach— at the chairs, at the couch, at the carved leg of a table.

A hoarse cry of terror was forced from him, and he awoke from the kind of stupor in which he lay, to find Dorothy standing, lovely and calm, at his side, holding in her hand a silver goblet filled with iced lemonade. He drew her towards him, and kissed her cheek.

Warmth, regret, and affection were conveyed in his embrace.

Dorothy, on her part, had been all day torn by conflicting emotions. She loathed herself for having broken the promise and missed her rendezvous with Joynte. She pictured to herself his rage and disappointment. She remembered that he had called himself a desperate man, and she dreaded lest harm should come to Keith from his revenge. She had obeyed her husband, indeed ; but at what a cost of suffering and self-respect ! In addition, she was sorely tormented by the knowledge that there did exist a secret which she was to be debarred from knowing, and about the guilt of which, spite of all efforts, she could not prevent feeling some suspicion.

Keith was her idol. She had thought him faultless. Was he to prove as erring as any other mortal ? The most perfect love is not blind ; it does not worship impossible images of fantasy, but yet its idol *is* of pure gold, unalloyed, and refined in the ardent and searching fires of charity and forbearance. Dorothy had not yet attained to such a love. Hers was still a very human passion, in which she beheld the reflection of the Ideal rather than the more sorrowful picture of the Real.

But even as she stood by Keith's side and heard the anguished cry which was the cause of his awaking, and looked upon his deathly face, perturbed and distressed out of his habitual calm, and felt his hand clasp hers and drag her down to him, and his lips fix one long kiss upon her cheek, she knew he loved her, and her heart grew light.

'Keith,' she whispered, 'when may we go home ?'

'Are you home-sick ?' he asked kindly.

'Not exactly; but still, I should like to go home—to Blackness—to the lovely room filled with books, and to the fairy lake ; and to all the peace and beauty.'

'Would you really like it ?' he said thoughtfully.

'Oh yes, indeed! Would not you ?'

'I will see if it is possible,' he said, kissing her again.

His words filled Dorothy with a great happiness. She loved Venice ; its poetry and picturesqueness appealed vividly to her imagination, but the associations which clung about it were sad and agitating. Her jealousy, her fear, her suspicions, had taken their birth here in this city of dreams, hanging between sea and sky; whereas in England—her own homely England—she might hope to find more lasting peace.

'I should not be surprised if our friend Chester had met with some annoyance,' said Palis to the Darlingtons, when Mrs. Chester had retired to attend her husband. 'He has seemed considerably preoccupied lately.'

'I only hope he will not make Dorothy unhappy, for she is such a dear girl,' said Lady Darlington softly, feeding her pug with bits of buttered cake.

'They understand one another, I think,' said Palis again.

'I can't fancy a man caring to live abroad when there is no necessity, especially in such a place as this, where there is neither sport, political life, nor anything else to amuse him, and when he has a nice little property at home,' interposed Lord Darlington sagely. 'Blackness is not a large estate, but he has plenty of ready money.'

'Yes, but he has no ambition,' said Palis quickly; 'which is the more to be regretted, because he is clever enough to keep the *Universal Review* going alone. You have no idea how well he can write; and he knows a great deal, thanks to his diplomatic career and all the worldly wisdom he has acquired.'

'He knows most about pretty women, I should imagine,' said Lord Darlington sarcastically, whose wild oats had been quickly if generously sown. 'Now, women are all very well in their way—you need not listen, my dear' (little Lady Darlington immediately opened wide her ears, and listened with all her might)—'but they can't occupy a man's whole life; he must have something to do besides. Now, it strikes me that Chester has not a thought beyond paying compliments to ladies and playing the violin.'

Lord Darlington had a great contempt for musical men. His mother, when he was a schoolboy, insisted on his being taught music; and as the cultivation of it shortened his playtime by half an hour, he naturally and very properly took a hatred to the art. However, he succeeded *nolens volens* in learning his notes, and actually got as far as to play 'Nelly Bly' with one hand fairly correctly, when he had the good fortune to catch one finger in a rat-trap and chop off a piece of it, which afforded him a valid excuse for dropping the obnoxious study. His lordship's soul could scarcely be said to 'discourse sweet music;' he did not object to Lady Darlington's feeble performance of 'I cannot sing the old songs,' 'Annie Laurie,' and 'The place where the old horse died,' in the long winter evenings, when he reposed in his armchair with the newspaper spread across his knees, and his eyes shut. It gave a pleasant finish to the hard day's hunting, and the little lady's sweet piping voice lulled him to sleep and put him in a good humour; but as for listening to a sonata or seeing a man sit down, when he wasn't paid for it, conscientiously to play Chopin's Preludes or Beethoven's Sonatas, his lordship said it was simply sickening. Chester played the violin without much execution, but with a sweet sympathetic tone and finish of expression which delighted the ladies and made Lord Darlington irate. This fact, indeed, accounted for his lordship's unusually severe strictures upon his friend's tastes.

'Chester ought to go into Parliament,' said Palis. 'That is his place; he has a knack of speaking.'

'What is he—a Liberal, I suppose? There, you know, I can't sympathize. I am strongly Conservative. What are you?'

'Sometimes one thing—sometimes another,' said Palis, laughing; 'whatever my paper happens to be. It is such a comfort to write anonymously; no one knows what your personal views are. You know, our journal leads public opinion; that is to say, we carefully notice which way the wind blows, and trim our sails accordingly. But I'm so devoted to Keith—next to Hugh Vennaker, he is my greatest friend—that I really would write him up if he took to public life, whatever his opinions.'

'Is there any chance of it, do you think, Mr. Palis?' said Lady Darlington eagerly. 'It would be so nice if he were a Conservative; you know it is really and truly more *respectable*. But now, as we are talking about Mr. Chester,' she continued, her curiosity getting the better of her manners, 'do tell us what was the queer story once circulated about him, which Dorothy told me was very nearly the cause of their marriage being broken off.'

'I really know nothing precise whatever,' said Palis quickly, loyal exceedingly; 'some previous entanglement, I believe.'

'Is the lady alive, then?'

'Oh no; she is dead—and left him her fortune.'

'Well, but there can be nothing disgraceful in that. What could people mean? was she not a lady?'

' Perfectly so; a charming American girl.'

' Well, then?' Lady Darlington interrogated impatiently.

' Well? that is just what I say.'

' It is very strange,' mused the little lady. (Lord Darlington, meanwhile, had fallen asleep.)

' Yes; it is very strange. Keith is a good fellow.'

' A capital fellow,' echoed his lordship, waking up, and chiming in vaguely. ' Who said he was not? Rides well to hounds, too.'

The more Lady Darlington thought it over, the more she felt convinced that some great mystery underlay Keith's existence, and the more, with that rapacity for excitement frequently to be found among people who neither read nor write novels, did she long to discover the solution.

' We must really take Dorothy home with us,' she remarked to her patient husband, as he stretched his long limbs beside her in the gondola.

' Not without *him*, my dear,' he answered.

' Oh, of course not without him! No one could wish to separate husband and wife; but I am convinced the air of Venice does not agree with either of them. A man ought

16—2

not to have that queer kind of sudden headache, and she looks worn to death.'

'Do you think she will look better in
England?'

'Certainly. I can keep an eye on her there
—the horrid Marchesa will be out of the
way—and you will insist on his going out
hunting every day. No one can be ill who
takes plenty of exercise.'

This view of the matter commending itself
entirely to Lord Darlington's approbation, he
dropped all further opposition, and with it the
subject of the Chesters' health, and fell to
talking of the latest news from Swivel.

'To think that I shall soon see Hetty and
Letty again!' said his wife ecstatically; 'I
shall be so pleased! I wonder if the darlings
are grown? We must take them a necklace
of those glass beads they make here, and then
they will look perfect cherubs.'

CHAPTER XVIII.

KEITH MEDITATES.

NEXT morning Keith felt no ill-effects from the previous night's indisposition. A trifle of languor perhaps oppressed him, and his eyes were rimmed with dark circles ; in other respects, he wore his ordinary appearance.

Dorothy, through her spectacles of tender love, scrutinized him carefully, but could find no ground for anxiety. However, the temporary fondness he had shown her had evaporated. He was no longer particularly affectionate, but quiet, composed, and somewhat abstracted.

After breakfast he left the house as usual, and paused for a moment, undecided in which direction he should bend his steps. He felt a remarkable distaste to the Marchesa's society this afternoon ; for, as he argued within him-

self, in reality she could not be compared to
his wife in youth, in beauty, or in freshness of
feeling. Her fascinating ways were but artificial, and savoured of trick; and he was not
quite sure that she was a real musician. Thus
musing, he pursued his way towards the cafés
of the Place St. Mark.

The air was balmy, the sky clear, yet he
experienced a lassitude of limb that affected
his spirits. What was the use of life ? what
was it worth? whither did it lead? To men
of idle self-indulgent habits there must come
such moments : moments when the game does
not seem worth winning, nor the brightest
gauds of ambition and glory to be aught but
lying shams. And yet Venice was lovely at
this moment : the wide expanse of lagune
stretched clear in the azure distance; cupolas,
tall and snowy, sparkled in the sun; the
laughter of girls echoed in the soft breeze;
windows suddenly opened let out snatches of
song, or the gay voices of men; the rhythmical
splash of the gondoliers' oars, their joyous
cries, spoke of life and gaiety, and of the fair
new hopes of each renewing day.

If he were to fall in the eyes of his wife, of
whose idolatry he was pleasantly conscious,
what a foolish, an uncalled-for degradation !

A few follies of youth—sins, if you like ;
yes, perhaps they were sins (but every young
man was guilty of them, after his degree)—
were destined to pursue him through life,
remorselessly and unaccountably. He shrank
from the publicity to be incurred, if he committed Joynte to his proper place, the mad-
house, as long as Judith, whom he had
believed dead, was there, a living witness
ready to proclaim the truth.

The truth! Was it the truth that surged
back upon his memory with waves of overwhelming force? that awful time in Rome,
when he was half-distraught with disappointment—the suspense, the misery, the end so
quickly consummated, then the long silent
hours of agony. Gradually the numbness of
reaction, hope reviving, forgetfulness bringing
its blessed balm, a fresh love—a glimpse into
a haven of purity and peace ; finally, an
anchorage of quiet domestic happiness. As
in a mirror, the various phases of his life
passed before his mental vision, revolving,
narrowing, concentrating round the follies of
his youth. Judith, the impersonation of those
follies, stood before his fancy again, with flashing eyes, pale, quivering lips, and cold revenge
speaking in her voice.

Perhaps, however, his wife, who loved him so well, who was so innocent and so gentle, would believe none of these things! A warm thrill of reviving hope passed through his veins; then her words flashed upon him, spoken firmly and honestly:

'I will not betray the poor man!'

Justice, then, was a stronger sentiment in her than love! Keith lifted his hand to his forehead. It was burning. The languor of his limbs had disappeared, and a feverish longing for change and active movement now possessed him. Fresh air and a swim would soon still these madly beating pulses. He hailed a passing gondola, and desired the man to convey him to the Lido.

It was late when Keith returned home, both mind and body thoroughly fatigued. Dorothy scarcely repressed a cry of dismay to see his hair still damp and blown about by the sea-breeze, his face pallid and drawn, his eyes unnaturally bright and febrile.

At dinner he became jocose and talkative, drank a good deal of wine, and entered into an argument with Lord Darlington on the subject of sport.

The guests having departed, Dorothy retired to her own room with a book. Keith and

Palis—the latter, as usual, overwhelmed with
work, which he got through at nocturn and
erratic hours—sat up late in the night, smoking cigarettes and planning out copy for the
Universal Review.

' There, Keith,' he said; ' listen: all the
papers of Europe and America are to be
represented in it; every shade and degree of
opinion. No one is to be greater or less than
another—poet, priest, aristocrat, and Red Re-
publican are to say their say, and plead their
mission; no more dogmatism, no more hard-
and-fast lines of demarcation between class
and caste; the aristocracy of the mind, and the
democracy of social institutions, the com-
munism of the intellect, free and open compe-
tition, the great principle of co-operation
regulating everything; not a sham that will
not be exposed, not a vice that will not be
condemned, not a virtue that will not be
upheld, not a misery that will not be assisted
by the triumphal voice of universal enthusiasm.
The best of liberty, the truest of equality,
progress !'

Thus cried Palis, with a flushing cheek and
sparkling eye, lighting his thirteenth cigarette
while he dashed aside a pile of manuscript.

Keith felt no particular enthusiasm for the

cause of the *Review*—he did not care much for liberty, equality, and progress; but the thing served to distract his mind as well as anything else, and Palis's enthusiasm was catching. The little man, with his red curling beard, his bright blue eyes, and his almost feminine delicacy of skin, had such a wonderful vitality, such an exuberant joyousness, such a perfectly transparent sincerity, that he carried away his auditors. His power of persuasiveness was probably the secret of his success, while his sense of boyish fun and perception of the ludicrous tempered the acrimony of his attacks and blunted the pungency of his sarcasm.

No one could dislike Palis, though few cared to depend upon him. From each he won a meed of admiration and regard.

CHAPTER XIX.

ILLNESS.

CIRCUMSTANCES never happen in exact accordance with our anticipations. Keith, on waking next day, tried to rise, and found himself too languid; tried to think, and was forced to confess himself incapable; tried to speak, and was interrupted by a nasty little cough.

Le Goui brought tea on a silver salver, and Dorothy sent for the doctor—a black-eyed dapper Italian, with a smell of garlic and snuff about him, who shook his head and prescribed an infusion of violet leaves.

'Is he seriously ill?' asked Dorothy, arresting the doctor as he took his departure through her boudoir.

The doctor pulled out his snuff-box, tapped

it, inhaled a pinch, sighed, blew his nose, and finally said :

' No, signora. It is a little feverish attack; it will soon pass. He must lie quiet, and drink the infusion I have prescribed.'

' Must he take no other precautions ? Can I do nothing ?'

The doctor looked approvingly at Dorothy's golden hair and gentle beauty.

' No; no other precautions are necessary. He will soon be well; but he must drink the infusion, and lie still.'

Such queer visions and fancies crowded in upon his brain and danced before his eyes, that Keith felt glad to lie still; and between his half-closed lids to see, in the subdued light, the tapestried gods and goddesses on the walls, and his wife sitting quietly, a little pensive, by the big dressing-table, laden with carved silver caskets and bottles. Indeed, to everyone in the palace, this illness seemed to bring relief: to Keith, who was glad to give up puzzling and arguing himself over Joynte's demands or Judith's unreasonableness; to Dorothy, distracted from her private cares by the joy of proving herself a capable nurse, an office she had always been qualified to fill; to Lady Darlington, who was glad because she thought the fever would afford a powerful excuse for her friend's return with her to England; to Lord Darlington, who was glad because his wife was glad, and because he should soon see his beloved hounds.

Perhaps Palis felt more regret than anyone at the lack of Keith's co-operation in the business of the *Universal Review;* but no little worries preyed long on his perennial flow of spirits ; and, as a set-off, an inspiration had just reached his fertile brain—the idea of a stirring war-song, whose martial strains would serve to rally the readers of the *Review,* as the 'Marseillaise' stirred the heroes of the revolution. He hummed the melody about the house all the day long, and tried it in every key, and with all varieties of modulation, on the piano in the grand gallery, the tones of which were inaudible to Keith in his bedchamber.

This occupation, and the succeeding one of copying out, revising, and arranging, kept Palis happily employed for several days ; so that he scarcely noticed how the time flew by, nor that Keith, after swallowing an incredible quantity of violet-tea, and patiently lying still, as prescribed, had now entered upon his convalescence, and was able to resume his place at dinner.

The doctor still continued, however, to shake his head and look serious, privately imparting his fears to Dorothy, whom he now mentally qualified as *una donna solide*.

'Get him home'—so ran his whispered advice—'get him home. He is sure to have another attack if he remains here.'

Dorothy racked her brain vainly in the endeavour to find a potent argument for his departure, and finally decided to trust to the chapter of accidents.

'The Darlingtons leave us on Wednesday, you know,' she said, throwing out a little reconnaissance on the first evening Keith appeared at dinner.

Palis woke up from his musical dreams, and discovered, to his surprise, that Keith, though as gay as ever, had grown considerably thinner and paler.

'I think I shall travel with them,' he said; 'my chief wants me home. I have finished my work here, and should like to get my song printed.'

'Why, then, we shall not have a single English friend left!' cried Dorothy, in dismay.

'Let us make up a party, and travel home together,' suggested Palis, to whom all life appeared a kind of picnic, for which it was wise to make up a party. 'I am a capital traveller, Mrs. Chester, I assure you!'

'Are you?' said Keith, smiling. 'The only time we travelled together you were in a brown study—the throes of composition, I suppose—all the time. You forgot your luggage, forgot your watch, mislaid your passport; lost your hat, and my time, and your own ticket, and only succeeded in preserving from the general chaos an obese carpet-bag, whose sides, threatening every moment to burst, were tied up with string.'

'Which bag exists to this day.'

'I am sorry to hear it. From it you periodically extracted a Bologna sausage, a roll, and a lump of chocolate, with which you refreshed your inner man.'

'I never lost my temper among the articles you enumerated just now.'

'That is true; but you exercised mine. What strange fancies you had, too! I remember a Piedmontese youth with dazzling teeth and large brown eyes, and a couple of white mice, for whom you conceived a strange infatuation. I found you regaling him and his mice on cakes and fruit in the buffet.'

'Quite true. That fellow *could* sing. My dear Keith, he was a Mario in disguise. What a lovely voice he had! what eyes! and he was fresh, too, from his native village. Nature unadorned and unspoilt by the vices of civilization has, I allow, the greatest charm for me.'

'He was certainly unadorned—and partial to fleas.'

'Confess our journey was a pleasant one, after all.'

'It was pleasant,' said Keith musingly; 'it was so unorthodox and so comical. You kept me in a constant state of laughter, suppressed, unfortunately, most of the time by the exigency of circumstances—sometimes by your preternaturally polite attentions to old ladies with baskets and bundles, sometimes by your knowing stare at young ones, your peculiar conversations with guards, porters, cab-drivers, and shop-girls.'

'La comédie humaine,' said Palis, sighing, as he helped himself to cucumber. 'Mrs. Chester, does your heart direct you to England?'

'Oh yes, indeed!' she said eagerly; 'and Keith knows it—don't you, Keith?'

Keith threw a kindly glance at her. Since his illness he felt himself quite the model husband. He had accepted with the best of grace Dorothy's devoted attentions and unwearied care; the domestic hearth was now become his ideal, for Judith's reappearance had cured him for ever of platonic or even musical flirtations. He was quite sure now that it was not safe to be on friendly terms with any woman but his wife.

'Dorothy, you had better decide our plans,' he said magnaminously, seeing they were waiting for him, Jove-like, to pronounce his fiat.

'There can be no doubt, then. I pronounce at once for England,' said Dorothy quickly.

'Hurrah for England, its mists, its lawn-tennis, and its pretty women!' said Palis, breaking into the familiar strain of his beloved war-song.

'Perhaps, however, the doctor will not allow me to travel yet,' said Keith doubtfully, feeling, like all men, as thoroughly nervous about his health, now he had taken the alarm, as he had been reckless and careless before.

'The doctor has prescribed it,' said Dorothy gaily; 'and I was already at my wits' end how to carry out his instructions without opposing your wishes.'

'Then, after all, I *have* a scheming little wife.' Keith looked at her, and smiled so cordially that the smile set her heart beating with exhilaration.

'Leave it to me, Keith,' she said—'leave it to me. You shall not have a minute's bother. I will arrange it all with le Goui. We will take him and Trimmer and the cook, and discharge the Italian servants. May I write to-day to Blackness, and order them to prepare the house—and to mamma and Margaret? What joy it will give them! Dear Keith; how good you are!'

Regardless of matronly dignity and of the presence of Palis, who discreetly fixed his eyes on the 'Bouchecs à la Reine' which he was eating, she jumped up and kissed her husband; but had only just time to resume her seat, with cheeks still rosy-red, when le Goui entered with the next dish, and observed her with his well-regulated eyes, which had learnt to see everything and notice nothing.

How happy Dorothy was in the next few days! She flew to her friend Lady Darlington, and confided to her all her hopes and her delight, and the truth that for a long period she had been really and truly home-sick.

She held consultations with le Goui—who had by this time accepted her presence in the household as an inevitable necessity, and was agreeably surprised to find out how much good sense on the whole she possessed, and, now that she had become more proficient in Italian, how cleverly she could manage the servants—as to the arrangements best calculated to promote Keith's comfort, and spare him fatigue on the journey. She paid off the household staff, and totted up bills with the ardour of an army controller; she visited cupboards, and turned out hidden nooks, and examined linen indefatigably. All this gave her the greatest satisfaction, and so changed the current of her thoughts that she even forgot Joynte, though he had taken care to remind her of his existence by a certain greasy note, in which he urged her good offices with her husband. She ran no risk of meeting him either, for she scarcely ever went out alone or on foot.

Keith was perpetually at home, and in her presence. He was so kind and gentle to her; he showed such trust and such approval of her doings; he grew so dependent on her society; he went out so meekly for a daily airing in the gondola; he lay so peacefully

all day, in his state of indolent weakness, on
the sofa in her boudoir, smoking and reading
French novels, that the conviction crossed her
mind that never, not even in the intoxicating
days of honeymoon and courtship, had she
tasted such perfect happiness. Keith seemed
so entirely her own, in bodily presence, in
heart and in inclination.

She mused thus one evening, sitting at the
large dressing-table, by the glimmer of two
stately wax-candles set in silver candlesticks,
while Trimmer, in a flutter of joy at the idea
of returning to her native land, brushed out
her hair. The heavy locks were spread out
to their full extent, and when the brush re-
treated in its regular movement they flew
back into curling waves, till they covered her
shoulders with a veil of gold.

'Nothing again could disturb their married happiness,' so ran her reflections. 'They
understood one another now; Keith knew
how much she loved him, and he loved her
dearly in return. How foolish she had been
ever to disquiet herself concerning the Marchesa, who was musical and artistic, and
naturally interested Keith in their mutual
tastes. Certainly only a wild imagination
could have read harm where there was none,

and mistaken common courtesy for foolish
dalliance. Venice might yet have only pleasant recollections in her memory. True, the
mosquitoes were troublesome, and Joynte's
behaviour had caused her uneasiness ; still, sal
volatile for the former, and perfect trust in her
husband for the latter, afforded satisfactory
alleviation. She would certainly regret the
charm of moonlight nights and the superb
colouring of brilliant days, and all the varied
delights of a life composed of sensation only,
of a perpetual feast of eye and ear. England
would probably seem cold and chill in the
contrast ; but England was her home, and
there lived her mother and Margaret, and
there were still the scenes and surroundings
of her happy childhood.'

Her reflections were interrupted by Trimmer's voice, tired of mechanically lifting and
dropping her arm without any responsive
notice from her lady.

'Dear me, ma'am ! how strange it will seem
to tread a peninsula again after living in the
water.'

'An island, Trimmer,' corrected Dorothy,
scarce able to restrain her laughter, for very
little things made her laugh just now.

'Well, I'm sure, ma'am, it's all the same

—some foreign word or other it is that means
dry land; not but what land never is very
dry in England without a deal of drainage.
Is Blackness a damp place, ma'am?'

'I don't think so. I have lived in the
neighbourhood all my life.'

'I only ask because Lady Mandrake always
passed the best part of the autumn at the sea-
side, and I have not been accustomed to the
country at that season, and the mist and
damp; though I'm perfectly sure I shall get
used to it, for I've a very strong constitution.
With Lady Mandrake we always used to have
a large house by the sea, and a deal of company visiting; for you see, ma'am, there's
folk who have not got much money of their
own, and so profit by other people's, and
live at the expense of a great lady. To
be sure, they must do many things that are
irksome, walk when they are tired, talk when
they'd like to sit still; but, as I always say,
"each one must earn his bread." The one
earns it by the sweat of his brow in the fields,
the other in a hot ball-room; but the bread
that's earned is the same, for all that.' Here
Trimmer brushed again more vigorously.
'Why, there was my lady's daughter, who
was married and a widow, and came home to

live with her. I've seen her ready to drop,
with talking to this one and that one, and
receiving company, while Lady Mandrake
slept in her chair ; and sometimes she would
come running up to her room and say, " Now,
Trimmer, there's a dear, fetch me a cup of tea
—strong, mind, for I'm very tired." I'd fetch
it in and welcome — for I'm not proud—if
the housemaid would just leave it at the door
and give a little tap, so as I should know it
was there. Then just when the poor lady was
a-setting down like comfortable to her tea, we
would hear my lady's bell ringing sharp,
and the footman come up and say, ' Please,
ma'am, there's company in the drawing-
room ;' and down would go the poor lady
without a word, and the bread and butter,
which Mrs. Tubbs had cut special fine and
wafer-like, untouched. And I'd say to the
housemaid, as I folded up the dresses, " Jane,
she's earning her bread like one of us, and a
hard job she has of it." '

' You are right, Trimmer ; there is a great
deal of drudgery in fashionable life,' said
Dorothy sweetly.

' Lady Mandrake got her money's worth
out of her, too. She certainly gave her board
and lodging, which she had no call to do ; but

then she tormented her in a sly way. She'd
make her get up early to write notes, and sit
up late to answer them. "Maria," she'd say,
"you're younger than I am; you've younger
legs than I have." And she'd go on so, till
she nearly ran her off those young legs.
"I'm glad I'm only a servant, Jane," I said,
sometimes; "for when I've done my work,
I've no need to be nagged at, and I can draw
a quiet breath, and read the *Family Herald;*
and I ain't got to think who is to be asked to
the next tea-party, and what single man would
do to make up fourteen at dinner." For my
lady was superstitious, ma'am, very, with all
her masterfulness. Are there ghosts at Blackness?' asked the garrulous lady's-maid, running off in a new sequence of ideas.

'Ghosts! None that I know of,' said
Dorothy, as she dismissed her attendant.
Ghosts! what ghosts could there be in a
cheerful house, inhabited by a pair of married
lovers?

Ghosts meant remorse and secrets, and dark
and bitter days; and how could there be any
such things at Blackness, where the only
ghosts were pictures of ancestors and ances-
tresses, all quietly laid to sleep in the family
vault, all accommodated with their monu-

mental brasses and complimentary epitaphs,
the very names and pedigrees of which breathed
respectability and decorum. No dark fore-
shadowings hung over Mrs. Chester; no regrets
disturbed her. She was young, innocent, and
beautiful ; there was no place in *her* cupboard
for a skeleton.

CHAPTER XX.

AT HOME AGAIN.

THE sleepy village of Dronington was roused into the liveliest state of excitement. Triumphal arches of pink calico and laurel spanned the main—in fact the only—street; from the linendraper's (the general bazaar and universal emporium), the grocer's and the butcher's shops flags and banners waved, bearing the mystic words, 'Welcome Home,' 'Happiness,' 'Long Life to the Bride and Bridegroom,' while the surprising variety and number of the colours and devices must have dazzled and astounded the unwary stranger, had any such passed by.

It was not every day that Dronington had the happiness of receiving a rich young squire and his bride, thus combining the gaily matrimonial, dear to the hearts of ladies, with the loyally conservative, precious to the farming and labouring interest. True, Mr. and Mrs. Chester were not personally popular ; he had resided abroad, and she had lived so quietly at home, having little to spend on charity or pleasure, that no time or opportunity had hitherto been given for the cultivation of any warm personal feeling on the part of society or dependents ; yet a halo hung around the couple—the halo of wealth and good-fortune— which in society irresistibly engenders respect, tempered by affection.

It was the rural and universal belief that now Blackness possessed a resident and gene- rous squire (for if he were rich and resident, he might be likely to prove generous) the country people could expect a future of prosperity.

Mrs. Parkinson naturally became one of the most energetic and active of the decorative committee, which she raised to a mission of love ; and Mrs. Maynard and the other ladies of the parish, carried away by her enthusiasm, proved capable helpers.

Tears stood in Mrs. Strait's eyes at these tokens of her daughter's importance. The slight difficulties and misunderstandings that had preceded the marriage were blotted out of her memory and comfortably forgotten, insomuch that aspersions on Mr. Chester's character would have now astonished no one more than herself.

Margaret, happy and unconcerned, carried her head higher, bought a new gown with cherry ribbons, and laughed a good deal more than the occasion seemed to warrant. Her sister had certainly mentioned, in the letter announcing their return, that Keith's illness was the immediate cause of it, and that he was not equal to much fatigue ; but Margaret reflected that no one able to travel could fail to be gratified by, or object to, rejoicings and congratulations on his behalf. So she joined the band of hard-working ladies with consideable alacrity, twisting wreaths and inventing designs for garlands and decorations to the best of her ability.

Another source of pleasure was afforded her by the permission to roam about Blackness and give orders, to inquire of the housekeeper as to the state of the larder, and to impress upon her that plenty of plums must be put into the cakes baked for tea. There was a charming sense of responsibility in all this, mixed with a diverting contempt of consequences. She held long discussions with the obliging Mrs. Nutmeg as to the respective merits of the tapestry or the red damask chamber for the use of the invalid—Margaret inclining to the tapestry-room, which possessed blue satin hangings and a fine view of the lake and fairy island, and Mrs. Nutmeg thinking the red damask more comfortable and appropriate, because it owned the finest bed. Eventually, Margaret carried the day, and the tapestry-room was decided upon. Mrs. Strait passed her time in examining the embroidery on the pillow-cases, which had been executed in an Irish nunnery, and was astonishingly elaborate; and thus matters progressed until the morning of the day that was to bring home Mr. and Mrs. Chester.

'There, that will do, I am sure.' Margaret, with due satisfaction, settled the bunch of roses and heliotrope she had just brought from the garden in a queer shaped Venetian glass, and stood a little way off, the cherry ribbons waving merrily with each movement of her head and hands, to examine the result of her labours.

'There, now, if Keith is not satisfied, I am sure he ought to be—blotting-case, papers, inkstand, flowers, books, all complete. Will he smoke, I wonder? Well, if he does, here is a pretty little saucer to hold the ashes, and he has a nice view, and all the sun. Mrs. Nutmeg, don't you think Mr. Chester will be very comfortable? I should like to sleep in that bed with the big frilled pillows and the blue satin counterpane. What a lovely counterpane.'

'Mr. Chester brought it himself from Italy,' said the fat housekeeper; 'they seem to spend a deal more trouble on their beds there than we do; but I reckon they don't sleep any better, with their fevers and their agues and what not. Poor dear master, I hope he is better, though he will be wanting possets and teas still, I suppose.'

'I hope so, too. Men soon pick up, I think, though I've always heard they are the worst invalids possible. Hark! What is that? It's —oh, it's the carriage!—let us run, or we shall be too late.'

In another moment Dorothy was clasped in the arms of her sister, who had flown out all smiles and cherry ribbons to welcome her. Mr. Chester looked pale and feeble as he stepped from the hired landau, drawn by a pair of horses, supplied for all ceremonies— weddings, elections, funerals, or party-going (open or shut according to the weather), by the landlord of the Seven Stars. Margaret was at no loss for exclamations.

'Well, you're home again, that's a comfort; and what a set of ghosts you look, too; poor dear Keith! can't he walk without a stick? Come in here; tea is ready in the library (if you don't mind going upstairs), and *such* a good cake—I superintended the making of it myself! Dorothy, you are as fresh and clean as if you had not been travelling.'

'We only came from London, to-day, you know,' said her sister, smiling, while Margaret twined her arm in Dorothy's and overwhelmed her with caresses; 'but Keith is very tired, the journey from Italy was so long and tedious.'

Here Margaret surprised a mutual loving look from the pair, full of tender yearning on Dorothy's and reassuring trust on Keith's part, and immediately decided within herself that she would on no consideration whatever be an old maid. In audible tones she said, however, something quite different.

'I am so sorry you are tired, because you really will have to go into the village to-morrow, and show yourself, and admire the triumphal arches; those you saw on your way from the station were nothing—we have all worked so hard, and are so pleased to see you.'

Margaret again kissed her sister, but Keith sank wearily into a chair. This movement drew Margaret's attention to him.

'You are to have the tapestry-room, you know, Keith, and it is very comfortable.'

'Why, that is the best room in the house, and I have *never* slept in it.'

'All the more reason you should,' replied Margaret, making a little ·courtesy; 'as you are the master of the house, and an invalid now. But this is a special occasion; you are to get well quickly, you know, and not imagine this a precedent for the future. You are only allowed to be ill once in a way.'

'Very well; but in that case you will have to come and nurse me when I am ill!'

Margaret tossed her head gaily, and flitted over to where Dorothy stood talking in a quiet business-like way to Mrs. Nutmeg.

'You will stay and dine—you and mamma? Oh yes, you must; I will take no denial!'

Dorothy laid her hand kindly on her mother's shoulder. Mrs. Strait was in a highly hysterical state of tears and delight.

'Mrs. Nutmeg, we shall be four; and please let us have dinner early.'

' Doesn't she give her orders well?' remarked
Mrs. Strait admiringly. ' I declare, Dorothy,
you have grown fat, and carry your self
better; I used to be afraid you stooped a
little.'

' How delicious to think we need fear no
mosquitoes to-night!' irrelevantly said Dorothy,
giving vent to a sigh of relief; ' they used to
worry Keith so when he was ill.'

' In your own palace?' said Margaret, with
astonishment. ' I. thought a palace must be a
kind of enchanted place!'

Dorothy smiled a little sadly. The enchant-
ment had but too quickly evaporated, leaving
in its stead a bitter sense of disillusion.

' Oh yes! mosquitoes and everything disagreeable! Venice was dreadfully hot; now
this place is perfection!'

' It feels damp,' said Keith, shivering. ' I
really think a fire would be pleasant.'

' In August!' cried the astonished Margaret.

' Why not? In this variable British climate
one can endure a fire all the year round, and
keep the window open if one is too hot.'

' But only look at the flowers; and a little
later on there will be a moon. Look at all
these beautiful geraniums, and lobelias, and
calceolarias, and the bed of heliotrope, and the

late roses, and then think of a fire! I see you will import all your foreign chilliness here; and, I declare, Dorothy, you dress differently. Well, I like that: your gown is prettily looped up. Trimmer must arrange mine for me; you won't mind, will you, dear?'

Margaret looked pleading, and Dorothy willingly gave her consent.

The dinner was a lively affair, and a source of constant surprises and laughter. The grand cook had not yet arrived; but Mrs. Nutmeg and the kitchen-maid improvised a charming meal; and le Goui, equal to all emergencies, brought up the champagne perfectly iced.

Margaret enjoyed herself as she had not done for months; the little epicure loved good cheer and luxury. Keith looked on languidly, and could hardly eat the roast grouse Mrs. Nutmeg's forethought had provided. Dorothy had made a little toilette, and, with her pretty cheeks somewhat flushed, presided at the table in a condition of supreme happiness.

They had parted with the Darlingtons in London; Palis had returned to his *Universal Review* and his literary duties; the Marchesa and her musical proclivities had been left far

behind in shadowy translucent Venice, and
Dorothy was once more with her own people.
She looked at all the loved faces with devout
and thankful joy—at her husband's finely
chiselled features, her mother's familiar droop
and weary worn face, at Margaret's affectionate
and beaming countenance, and she felt her
heart expand with thrills of wonderful
gratitude.

Le Goui moved with velvet tread about the
airy dining-room, filling up the glasses, and
handing round a dish of late strawberries; and
as she watched it all—the pleasant home-like
scene, the flowers, and the fruit, and the
friendly ancestors benignly looking from the
walls—it came to Dorothy to wonder what
good things earth could give that she did not
already possess, except, perhaps, a little baby
face nestling in her lap. Well, there was
time enough for that!

It was not late when the party separated.

Mrs. Strait and Margaret intended to walk
home attended by a man-servant; and it was
felt that the abnormal effervescence of high
spirits could not be expected to remain long
at high pressure. Keith, too, was an invalid,
and kept early hours.

The last ringing tones of Margaret's voice,

dispensing good-byes and good wishes to the company, ceased to resound gaily in the air; and by the small fire that had been lit agreeably to Keith's desire in the library, Dorothy and her husband now sat waiting till le Goui should summon him to rest with the announcement that all was ready.

'What a happy day it has been, Keith!' she said, drawing a small stool near, and seating herself at his feet; 'everything so pleasant—you at home again and nearly well, for you will be rested to-morrow. I think *this* and our wedding day are the red letters of my life. How homely everything is! The books and their dear old covers, and your mother's pretty china, and the looking-glass and velvet. You will say it is bad taste; but I like it far better than that old tapestry, which always seemed to suggest something mysterious and uncomfortable and weird.'

'There is tapestry in my room here,' said Keith, whose face had grown pallid as he warmed his hands at the blaze.

'But it is quite different; only just a piece in a frame, and the subject is gay; no one could have gloomy fancies in that blue satin-lined bed, I am sure.'

Keith, in his capacity of invalid, soon retired

to rest, but Dorothy felt too happy for sleep.
She moved in blissful restlessness about the
dressing-room opening into Keith's room,
which she had appropriated in order to ensure
a prompt attendance to his wants, singing
softly to herself, moving little things upon
the table, glancing at the prints upon the wall.
Then, true to her old habit, she opened the
window and looked out.

The terrace, dotted here and there with jars
of feathery palms or drooping fuchsias, lay
peacefully steeped in the golden light of the
harvest moon, whose rays glittered on the still
waters of the lake. The scene had all the
beauty of Venice, with none of its sadness—the
sadness of ruin and decay. Here there was a
smiling garden, ample foliaged trees, telling
of plenty and content.

She heaved a happy sigh, and busied herself
again about the room. Presently she heard a
faint sound from Keith's chamber, as though
some one were calling. She opened the door.
Keith's voice, grown a little querulous, reached
her.

'I can't sleep; I am too hot. Will you
move the counterpane and give me some
orange-flower water to drink?'

'Oh, Keith, I am so sorry! you finished

the last bottle yesterday, and I fear there is no more unpacked. Shall I call le Goui?'

'No; let the poor fellow rest. He has worked hard enough all this week. But it *is* very vexatious. I shall never sleep, I expect.'

'Would you like anything else?'

Dorothy removed the counterpane thoughtfully. If Keith could not sleep, he would be so tired to-morrow.

'Stop! let me see! Yes; I have an idea I put a bottle of orange-flower water in that cabinet with the old-fashioned brass handles, in the corner. It stood in my bedroom when I was last here. I can't think why Mrs. Nutmeg moved it. Here is the key, on my watch-chain, and the inside part unlocks with my key-ring. Open it and look.'

Dorothy did as she was desired, and found the bottle. When she had poured out a glass of water, and he had taken a long draught, he said:

'There, that is better. Thank you, dear; that will do now; and by-the-bye, as you have opened the cabinet, find a paper which I shall want to-morrow. It will save me trouble to have it handy. It is the draft of an agreement about a farm, and there are a couple of letters

on the subject. Find them all, and put them
on the table.'

'There are a good many papers,' said
Dorothy, rummaging in the cabinet. 'Shall
I look them all through?'

'Yes,' he said wearily, closing his eyes.

In the indistinct flicker of the candle, which
she was forced to hold in one hand while she
turned over the papers with the other, she
found it almost impossible to decipher the
writing; so she hastily gathered up all the
papers in a heap, in her gown, and took them
into her room to examine at leisure, by the
light of her lamp. Keith seemed drowsy, and
her presence might drive away the precious
boon of sleep.

The papers were a queer medley. First
she found Keith's certificate of baptism, and a
packet of letters from his mother, written in
a faded, ladylike hand, on paper brown with
age; these she handled respectfully, pausing
over the simple, motherly terms of endear-
ment addressed to 'her darling boy.' Next
she found a half-torn French novel of Balzac's,
treasured for some mysterious reason ; printed
lists of companies, a game-license, the pro-
spectus of a wine merchant, an old diary of his
boyhood, and a packet of sweet-smelling

pastilles, all evidently tossed carelessly in to keep them out of the way.

She turned the things over more and more impatiently. What a quantity of trash—treasured trash, too! Keith must have made a mistake, the lease could not be here. It did not seem like a receptacle for business papers at all. Then came a few more unimportant letters, and that was all. Dorothy gathered them together and stole back softly to replace them in the cabinet. Perhaps she had left some behind inadvertently. She glanced at the bed with the idea of appealing to Keith, but his breathing was quiet and regular. He was sleeping at last.

She looked again more carefully to see if any receptacle had been omitted in her search, passing her hand in the semi-obscurity gently up and down, and into all the crannies. In so doing, her fingers pressed against a button, and a small drawer flew open. In it was a leather case, and a bundle of papers. Fancying she had attained her object, she again crept back, leaving the door, as before, slightly ajar. She drew a small chair up to the table, seated herself, and began methodically to untie the ribbon which bound the documents, and to unfold them one by one. As she did so, she noticed that they were chiefly letters—love-letters—and signed ' Ida.'

Then immediately her observation was drawn to the leather case. Opening it, she found that it contained a miniature—the likeness of a handsome young girl, with bright beaming eyes, quantities of light auburn hair, and a high-spirited expression. Beneath was written, in flowing gold letters, ' Ida.' It was the portrait of Ida—of the girl who had loved him, left him a fortune, and was dead. Was she on the brink of the mystery of which Joynte had spoken ? Should she know all ? How handsome the face was ! how fine the delicately aquiline nose ! how high-bred the upward curve of the nostril ! It was the face of one who would love to rule ; yet she was dead. Peace to her memory !

Dorothy closed the case reverently. She felt no petty jealousy, but rather a tender pity and gentle curiosity. Next came the turn of the letters, which she seized with feverish haste. Love letters ! she herself had never written any; her romance had been so short; but Ida had turned in another page in the book of love. From one of the letters, as she unfolded and read them, there fell a piece of foolscap paper, scrawled over in a man's hand.

Dorothy's eyes but too rapidly seized the meaning of the writing ; and, as she did so, the paper dropped from her shaking hand, and her head fell forward on the table.

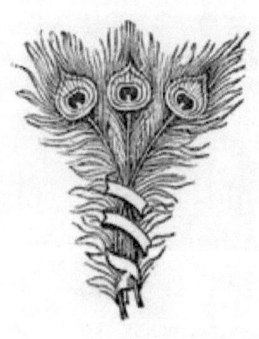

CHAPTER XXI.

A DISCOVERY.

IT was some minutes before Dorothy recovered from the stunned condition into which she had sunk, sufficiently to summon her energies to the further perusal of the paper. For a little while she gently fluttered some stray leaves of the letters, and read a few of the passages. At first, they were only unstudied outpourings of a girl's ardent love, more broadly and unguardedly expressed than is perhaps usually considered orthodox; yet their very frankness revealed their innocence. They ran through the whole gamut of passion, beginning in the simple major of true friendliness, warming, deepening, till they swept along, striking complex chords of ardent affection; presently they turned into the plaintive minor of self-distrust and humility, till with a crash of sharp discords the storm of jealousy and passion was ushered in. Such tender phrases as, 'You have grown so precious to me;' 'My eyes hunger for a sight of you. I could fain tell you so over and over again; and yet I *can't* turn my heart into words;' 'My garden is so beautiful: sweet scents are in all the air. Oh, to have *you* here to make it perfect!' were succeeded by cries of misery, of jealous desire so acute, that Dorothy's heart died within her. 'I have a wild longing upon me,' Ida said once, 'to be near any river or water that is rushing away somewhere—anywhere, and is not stopped, like a lake, by earthen banks; a swift, stealthy-rushing river, strewed with amber froth, hurrying on to that future, which sometimes seems a deep, dark sea, in whose bosom lies the storm—sometimes the clearest crystal mirror. I thirst to be loved, and crave to hear your voice;' then followed pages of wild and bitter reproach, and harsh upbraidings; then again softening streams of tenderness, 'I *cannot* give you up: I am *so* fond, and *so* weak.'

Finally came a short cold note: 'You have deceived me unworthily. I will never see you again!'

But though this human tragedy, played out
thus intensely before her eyes, moved Dorothy
as with the sight of some new world of strong
emotion and undisciplined feeling, carrying her
out of her own little narrow sphere of homely
love and duty, still it was the letter on the
piece of foolscap paper, the letter written in
long scrawly uneven lines up and down the
page, blotted here and there as though composed in the heat and hurry of passion, that
iced her blood and made her hands tremble.
She glanced at the signature. Her forebodings
had not deceived her. It was from Elias
Joynte.

'Scoundrel!' it began; 'plotting villain!
capable of stealing away one girl's affections
for the sake of her money, while you break
the heart of another; and not content with
that, even stoop to crime—to the cowardly
treacherous crime of murder, I am determined to denounce you and to hand you over
to justice. I was in the garden of the Villa
Peruzzi on that afternoon which decided
your fate. I saw all that took place, crouching in the bushes just under the long French
windows opening into the garden. I heard
Miss Phaer tell her servants she did not wish
to be disturbed, and lock her door on the

inside; then just as I was myself coming forward to speak, and reveal to her facts which your future wife ought to know, I saw you creep through the little garden-gate, to which you had a private key, Miss Phaer's own key, and I lay still and watched. I saw Miss Phaer greet you, somewhat surprised at the intrusion, looking like a lovely picture in her white morning-gown with blue ribbons, matching the snood that bound the chestnut hair which streamed all down her back. You evidently took her at a disadvantage; she had not expected you. You came nearer. Her eyes flashed, and her look was haughty. She reproached you. I could not hear the exact words, but not a gesture was wasted upon me. You lost your temper; she cried. Those beautiful eyes brimmed over with tears. Her passion rose, but *you* grew quieter and paler. You were nearly as pale as new ivory. She turned away then, and covered her eyes with her handkerchief.

'Having stung her, I suppose, to the quick, you poured yourself out a glass of water from the carafe that stood on the table. Into this you threw some liquid out of a small bottle, which you took from your pocket. A sudden exclamation from Miss Phaer, who still had her back to you, startled you ; instead of dropping the liquid deliberately in, your hand shook ; and all the contents fell into the glass. You quickly put the bottle into your pocket and walked to the window. Your face as you looked out straight at me, who was crouching, motionless and attentive, so near to you and yet invisible, was a study. You were haggard ; despair was written in your eyes. Presently you turned and saw Miss Phaer in her white morning-gown, her beautiful hair streaming down her back, quietly drinking the poisoned glass of water. Of course this was exactly what you wanted. You rushed towards her, pressed her in your arms, apparently to stifle her cries, for you never called for help. After a moment you laid her on the sofa, and flew as if the furies pursued you down the garden into the street, letting yourself out at the little gate, which you did not fail to lock, taking the key away with you.

'Miss Phaer was dead. I stayed some time watching her; she never moved. I climbed over the wall the way I had come myself (knowing otherwise I should have had no chance of being admitted into Miss Phaer's presence, for, as you remember, she had

quarrelled with me about you), and I was
glad and thankful to get out of the place.   No
one thought she had been murdered, no one
had seen the occurrence ; her door was locked
in the inside.   The glass and the prussic acid
accounted to her mother for everything, knowing, as she did, of her broken engagement,
consequent on the discovery of Judith's story.
To the outside world she died of heart-disease ;
but her death followed so quickly on the
rupture of her engagement to you, that the will
she made in your favour was never revoked.
You were rich, and you were free.   Was ever
anything more damnable ?—was ever crime
more profitable?   As soon as I discovered
this I determined how to act.   I saw you
to-day, and I told you that unless you at
once, and without demur, handed over to me
my cousin's fortune, I should denounce you.
You laughed, you sneered, said I could prove
nothing.   Very well—time will show.   I write
this detailed account of what I have seen, in
order that you should understand my power.
I give you till to-morrow at sunset ; if by
that time you do not send me your written
promise of restitution, you know the consequences.   I am a man of my word.   Choose!

' E. JOYNTE.'

On the margin of this terrible epistle was written, in Keith's clear small handwriting, the words :

' Elias Joynte, a dangerous lunatic, was, by my advice, confined in a madhouse that same day.'

The letter, with its marginal annotation, had evidently been forgotten; for it had lain among the folds of one of Ida's love-letters, where, except for the unfortunate chance of Dorothy's search, it would probably have rested for ever.

It seemed to Dorothy afterwards, looking back upon this awful time, as if she must have sat there motionless for hours. When she lifted her head at last, and looked around, the lamp had gone out, and the candle flared in its socket. She put her hand to her forehead, which ached with a dull pain; slowly, as in some horrible torture, the knowledge she had acquired stamped itself upon her brain. She began to cry out in agony, wringing her hands :

' My God—my God! not this—not this!'

Involuntarily the God neglected in our happy hours is earnestly invoked at moments of heart-rending trial; but no comfort came to her soul, only an utter loathing and revulsion from the surroundings of her luxurious life. Her husband a criminal—her riches a fraud! The very blue satin hangings, the soft yielding carpets, the carved furniture, acquired by sin and treachery! She tore the diamond rings from her fingers, and threw them on the table : she hated *them*—herself—everything.

In the next room lay Keith, the author of all this misery, unconscious of the drama being acted thus silently and cruelly in his vicinity; and through the door came—in the drear and solemn silence of the night, of those hours when birds are hushed and the spirit wakes—his gentle breathing—the breathing as of a tired child.

Dorothy moaned. They had been so happy lately; she had loved him so. And now, awful thought, could she ever love him again? ever bear to touch his lips with her pure lips ? to take his hand—the blood-stained hand of a *murderer*—in hers ?

The remaining years of her life must be a penance, an expiation, a cry for mercy to the throne of the Almighty. Was it possible that men could live, happily, frivolously, carelessly, with such an awful sin on their conscience? was there, perhaps, really no such thing as conscience and remorse? Her head swam, right and wrong mixed themselves in her mind. But oh! the wretchedness, the meanness of it all; did she even now know everything—who was Judith, and what was *her* story? Perhaps the very bitterest suffering to a proud spirit lies in the sense of deception, of having lavished despised treasures on unworthy objects, of having cast pearls before swine. Dorothy, with all her gentleness, encouraged self-respect bordering on pride; she had surrendered her heart into this man's keeping, she had chained her existence to his, and now she must suffer with him and through him. Through the long hours of the night the old fabric of happiness crashed and fell in ruins about her, and still the agony lasted, rising and falling in rhythmic phases of proud rebellion or dumb and helpless despair.

Silence overcame her at last, the silence of the heart and of the brain. She grew too exhausted to suffer: the strain and disruption had been so intense. Poor little unit battered about in the great churn of human misery, what were her woes that they should attract much attention? Thousands of other aching hearts that night ached in unison, thousands of proud spirits lay crushed in bitterness and self-abasement. Gradually the silence was broken by a tentative chirp, the darkness grew less dense, and the timid rays of light gathered strength, and rested on the golden head bent down in piteous agony. The glorious day returned in its beneficent course, and brought with it balm and peace. Dorothy slept.

END OF VOL. II.

BILLING AND SONS, PRINTERS, GUILDFORD AND LONDON.

S. & H.

www.ingramcontent.com/pod-product-compliance
Lightning Source LLC
Chambersburg PA
CBHW060601030726
47498CB00005B/1490

* 9 7 8 3 3 3 7 0 6 5 3 7 9 *